D1549886

FATHER DAN

Anthea Dove

Father Dan:
The story of an
Imperfect priest

the columba press

First published in 2009 by
the columba press
55A Spruce Avenue, Stillorgan Industrial Park,
Blackrock, Co Dublin

Cover by Bill Bolger
Origination by The Columba Press
Printed in Ireland by ColourBooks Ltd, Dublin

ISBN 978-1-85607-640-1

This book is dedicated to Chris,
who is not a priest, and not perfect,
but unquestionably 'the wind beneath my wings'.

Here I am, Lord. Is it I, Lord?
I have heard you calling in the night.
I will go, Lord, if you lead me,
I will hold your people in my heart.

Daniel Schutte, based on Isaiah 6

CHAPTER ONE

Canon Murphy died on Sunday night, peacefully in his sleep. Although at ninety-one his death was hardly un-expected, the parish of St Boniface was stunned and sad-dened by the news. People who had been cursing the canon for years remembered his good points: his piety, his gen-tleness with old people, his firm guidance in time of need. Letters of condolence and Mass offerings flooded in through the presbytery letter box and parishioners greeted each other with solemn faces.

'Just like him,' said William O'Connor reverently, 'to go to his Maker at the end of a busy day, preaching at three Masses, God rest his soul.' (The Canon preached at every Mass for fear of what the curate might come out with.) William himself, 85 years old, could see no fault with the Canon whom he had served on the sanctuary since his arrival at St Bon's as Father Murphy thirty years ago. Now he was standing in the presbytery with Mrs Macnab the housekeeper, helping her to sort out the Mass cards.

Edna Macnab nodded her agreement, and allowed a single tear to slide down her ruddy cheek. A stout woman and stern, she too had been a faithful servant to the Canon. But for her, his death had brought mixed feelings. He had been a tyrant and she had been a tyrant on his behalf, keeping at bay anyone who seemed in the least likely to threaten the Canon's serenity or his afternoon nap. But now she was tired and apprehensive. She'd had enough of this sort of life, eating her meals alone in the cheerless kitchen, feeling it unfitting for someone in her position to make friends in the parish. One or two of the women had

7

come to her with kindness and offers of hospitality, but Edna felt it her duty to keep herself to herself, and her forbidding countenance quickly discouraged any well-meant approaches.

She had been widowed very young and was childless. For twenty-three years she had worked for the Canon, loyal, lonely, unloved and unloving. Now she viewed the future with dread. She felt quite unable to cope with some young progressive priest who might take over the parish. But what was she to do? Where could she go? For a moment of weakness she wondered about confiding her worries to old William, but she pulled herself together in time.

'Huh!' she snorted, looking at the Mass card in her hand with its picture of cherubs and the message neatly written: 'In memory of the most wonderful priest, dear Canon Murphy.' 'Sentimental rubbish!'

William, given to a bit of sentimentality himself now and then, only raised an eyebrow. Edna Macnab had long since ceased to surprise him.

Upstairs in the same house Rupert Brownlow, the assistant priest, stood looking out of his window on to the railway line trying to sort out his feelings, trying not to rejoice.

It seemed like a miracle! He had made up his mind to go to the bishop on Monday, and the Canon had died just in time. Rupert had been at St Bon's for nearly a year. It was his first job as a priest and he had been absolutely determined to stick it out. Everybody, all his friends among the clergy, had commiserated with him on his appointment and told him nobody, not even the Bishop, would expect him to last more than six months. Only one man, Harry McHugh, had ever stayed with the Canon for more than a year and two had suffered breakdowns, one had left the priesthood, one had become an alcoholic and the rest had simply run to the bishop and begged to be moved.

Rupert was going to be different. He came to St Bon's on fire with enthusiasm, with love for the Lord and love of his people. He was going to love the Canon, no matter what. He was going to show them, the cynics. He was going to be like Harry McHugh.

But alas for Rupert, the Canon didn't seem to want to be loved. He wanted Rupert to do as he was told, and to be kept in his place. Rupert was not allowed to preach, or to make friends with the clergy of other denominations, or worse, with lay people. He was not allowed to start a prayer group. He was not allowed a television set or a record player in his room, or to drink alcohol, except on Christmas Day and Easter Day. His room was dismal in the extreme and without heating. Mrs Macnab's cooking was dreadful – ' plain and wholesome' the Canon often re-marked, though not to Edna herself – he didn't agree with praising people in case it made them proud.

And yet – on this Monday, this day of liberation when he didn't have to go to the bishop after all, Rupert felt a certain sense of loss. He remembered once hurrying out late at night in answer to an urgent call to find the Canon there before him in a squalid little council flat. He had stood in the doorway of the small room, sickened by the smells but uncertain what to do, and watched and listened as the Canon comforted the dying woman, with such pow-erful tenderness that Rupert was moved to tears. And an-other time he had slipped into church to pray and found the Canon there with a little girl (later he discovered she was his brother's granddaughter). He didn't notice Rupert, who stared incredulously at the old man's face, gentle, affectionate, happy even, as he had never seen it. He held the little girl's hand as he led her round the church, smiling and chuckling, 'like a normal human being' Rupert thought to himself.

Now he sat on his bed and prayed earnestly for the re-pose of the soul of Canon Murphy.

The laity, by and large, hadn't known the Canon as closely as his housekeeper and assistant. Everyone respected him for his integrity and single-mindedness and many people admired his rigid adherence to the letter of the law and the way he managed to ignore almost totally what he described as the 'new-fangled theology' which came in with the nineteen-seventies.

As people went about their business in the parish, they greeted fellow Catholics with sad expressions and spoke in subdued voices: 'Such a shock, wasn't it?' 'Such a good and holy man!' 'I'm taking the day off for the funeral.'

Only Kate Moriarty dared to be different, for such was Kate's way. Lydia Drew, President of the Catholic Women's League, had rung her up with the news.

'Kate, something awful has happened. Canon Murphy died in his sleep.'

'Thank God!' Kate said.

Lydia was shocked. 'Kate, you don't mean it ...'

'But I do,' Kate's voice over the phone was very firm. 'I do thank God. The Canon was ready to go, wasn't he? And we need a change here so badly. I'm sorry Lydia, but I can't help feeing delighted.'

The funeral was an impressive occasion. Among the Canon's orderly papers Rupert had found directions for the ceremony down to the smallest detail. He had found a copy of the will, leaving a substantial amount of money to Edna Macnab, enough to set her up comfortably for life.

The bishop came, of course, and so did the vast majority of St Bon's parishioners, including Kate Moriarty. The church was overflowing, the organ thundered and the congregation sang for all their worth (a stranger passing by assumed it was a Methodist chapel). The sermon was long and eloquent and the distant women relations flown over from Ireland wept copiously.

Afterwards, there was a grand tea provided by both the Catholic Women's League and the Mother's Union who had never been known to co-operate. Kate Moriarty, who belonged to neither, brought along an apple strudel and

some garlic bread. There was wine too (funds left specifically for this by the Canon) and when everyone was well
nourished the bishop, looking much happier now, made a
speech nearly as long as his sermon. His last words were:
'I expect you would like to know who the dear Canon's
successor will be. I have appointed Father Daniel Spring to
be your new parish priest. May God bless you all.'

Father Daniel Spring? Nobody had ever heard of him!
Even Wilfrid Drew, who represented the parish on the
diocesan council and had a finger in every Catholic pie,
had little to report about him, except that he had just come
back from working in South America and before that had
been studying in Rome.

'Doesn't sound too good to me', said Oliver Hardy, who
never failed to look on the black side. 'We need somebody
with experience of parish life, not some intellectual who's
spent all his life with his nose in a book!'

'I don't suppose he was entirely glued to books in
South America' said Kate Moriarty. 'I hope he's a liberation
theologian.'

'God save us, we don't need any sort of theologian!'
Norah McGinty exclaimed. 'We want someone with his
feet on the ground like the dear old Canon, God rest his
soul.'

'Well, let's hope he's not Irish!' Amanda Trumpington,
a diplomat's daughter, had somehow failed to inherit her
father's talents. 'It would be so good to have someone really
well educated. Father Rupert, poor lamb, is charming and
has such good taste. It will make such a difference to him
to live with a kindred spirit, don't you think, Mrs
McGinty?'

But Norah for some reason was stomping away. Old
William smiled at Amanda, 'I don't care if he's well educated, black or white,' he said, 'as long as he doesn't bring
guitars into the church.'

People who lived near the presbytery kept an eager

look-out, hoping to be the first to glimpse the new parish priest. But Father Daniel Spring eluded them all, arriving late on a Thursday night.

Father Rupert opened the door and smiled nervously at the stranger. 'Good evening,' he said. 'Hello! Rupert?' said the man, smiling broadly and gripping Rupert's pale thin hand in a strong handshake. 'I'm Dan Spring. Can I come in?' Rupert took a few steps backwards, trying to conceal his surprise. 'Oh yes, of course, Father,' he stammered. Father Spring followed him into the sitting room. 'Is there anything to eat?' he said, 'I forgot to get anything at dinnertime.'

Rupert blushed. 'I'm afraid I've just finished my fish and chips,' he said. 'I've been using the take-away since Mrs McNab – she was the Canon's housekeeper – left on Monday.'

Father Spring went into the kitchen. 'Have you some bread and cheese?' he asked and within minutes he had made himself a Welsh rarebit and was tucking into it with relish.

Rupert sat and watched him. He was Irish, of medium height and stocky build, neither handsome nor ugly but with an air of confidence and energy. He was wearing some old cords and a brightly patterned jumper. He looked comfortable, at ease, and yes – happy.

Rupert, who never took off his clerical collar and black suit except at bedtime, found himself almost liking this stranger who seemed so relaxed and cheerful.

He was smiling now. 'I feel a lot better for that' he said. 'Now would you show me round the house, Rupert, and then we can pray for a while.'

Rupert nearly said 'I've said evening prayer', but bit back the words in time and they began a tour of the house.

The dining-room, with it's stiff-backed chairs and dark red wallpaper had been the Canon's pride and joy. Father Spring shuddered and looked at Rupert. 'A bit gloomy isn't it? We can eat in the kitchen, can't we? And if we got rid of all this stuff,' he indicated the Canon's furniture, 'and got some easy chairs and painted the walls white, it would make it quite welcoming – for prayer groups and parish meetings – somewhere people could come and relax.'

The only remaining room on the ground floor was the waiting room. 'My God!' said Father Spring. 'If I had to wait in here I'd turn and run a mile. Wouldn't you?' He looked directly into Rupert's eyes, smiling again.

Rupert felt he had to be honest. 'I'm afraid I just accepted everything', he said, 'I never questioned it. The Canon ...' he fell silent, not wishing to be disloyal. 'Yes, I can guess,' said Father Spring, 'but we'll soon have this room looking bright and cheerful – it needs some fresh flowers and pretty curtains and I expect we can find someone in the parish who'd do us some paintings or drawings.'

Upstairs, Rupert showed Father Spring his room with some pride. The bed was perfectly made, everything was neat and tidy. But the new parish priest's reaction was not what he expected. He turned on Rupert a look of admiration. 'You don't mean you've slept in here for nearly a year and stayed sane?' he said. A train blasted past, rattling the window, filling the room with deafening noise, sending a cloud of dust and grit through the gap in the ill-fitting window. Father Spring looked at the brown linoleum and the dark brown curtains and bedcover.

'Surely there's another room you could have, Rupert? You can't like this?' 'Well, no, but I don't really mind,' said Rupert. 'There's the Canon's room – that'll be yours, of course' he added hastily, 'and then there's another big room but the Canon always kept that ready in case the bishop came. Oh, and there's Mrs McNab's room, that's bigger than mine and it's on the other side of the house.' 'What about upstairs again?' 'Well, there is a room up there, it's quite big, with dormer windows. It's full of old books and statues though.' Father Spring ran up the stairs and inspected the room in the attic. When he came down he said, 'Well, Rupert – which would you prefer – the attic or the Canon's room?'

Rupert, used to being accommodating, was about to say the attic room when he realised the man in front of him was full of surprises. 'I'd really love either,' he said, 'Which would you prefer, Father?'

'For heaven's sake, man, call me Dan. I'd prefer the attic. If the bishop does come he can have Mrs McNab's room. And I'd really like us to do up one of the rooms and make it our guest room. Then we can have our friends to stay, or family perhaps. What about your parents, Rupert? Are they still alive?' 'Oh yes, they're both fine, though my Dad is nearly sixty. He's a Church of England vicar.' 'Hey, that's interesting. I'd love to meet him. And what about your mother? Does she work?' 'No, not now. She used to be a librarian but she loves being retired. They still live in the village where I grew up. But yes, I'm sure they would come if I asked them.' 'Have they been here?' asked Dan. 'Well, no. The Canon thought it would be best if I didn't see them, not for my first year anyway, and especially with my dad being, well – you know….' 'Was your Dad very disappointed when you decided to become a Catholic?' 'I don't think so. He never said. But they came to my ordination and they seemed very happy for me.' Dan smiled. 'Now obviously we've got a lot of work to do. Are you any good with a paint brush?' A glance at Rupert's beautiful hands gave him the answer. 'Never mind – there's bound to be somebody out-of-work in the parish who'd jump at the chance. Now, let's go and pray.'

To Rupert's amazement, this tough, hearty, confident Irishman prayed as he had never seen anyone pray before. He sat close to Rupert and prayed first for the people of St Bon's, then for Rupert, then for himself. 'Lord, you know my weakness, my cowardice, my uncertainty – help me not to be afraid. Stay with me always.' After a silence, he looked up at Rupert. 'Now, tell me about the parishioners,' he said.

CHAPTER TWO

Next morning Rupert woke and smiled, realising he was in this bedroom for the last time. He actually enjoyed hearing his windows rattle as the express train for London roared by, but then he sat up with a start. What time was it? Surely that couldn't have been the nine o'clock train? His alarm clock confirmed that it was and he jumped out of bed and began to pull on his clothes. Then he noticed a smell, an enticing smell that he hadn't enjoyed since he was last at home a year ago, bacon frying, and surely, real coffee?

Fifteen minutes later, shaved but not showered, he ran downstairs and into the kitchen. Father Dan was there, laying the table. He grinned.

'Morning, Rupert,' he said, 'I don't usually indulge in more than a couple of slices of toast, but I thought I might manage my first day here better on a more substantial breakfast. I went out and found Sainsburys. It's a beautiful morning and it was good to be out.'

'I'm sorry ...' Rupert began.

'For what? You must have needed your sleep, lad. Now I'm guessing you and the Canon had all your meals in the dining room, but I find it a bit gloomy and certainly cold, so do you mind if we eat in the kitchen?'

The food tasted as good as it smelt and Rupert began to relax.

'Now let's get rid of these dishes and then you can start filling me in about the parish,' Dan said.

After they'd washed up the breakfast things, they sat down at the same table and Dan produced a writing pad and a pen.

'Right!' he said, 'I want to get a flavour of St Bon's from you. Tell me about the people.'

Rupert hesitated. 'Well,' Dan asked, 'do they seem happy in church? Are there lots of active groups in the parish? Are the lay people willing to be involved in running things? How are the young people involved? Is there a prayer group? A Justice and Peace group?' Seeing Rupert's worried face, he stopped. 'Sorry, I'm getting carried away. I'm not giving you a chance. Now you tell me how it is around here, and I'll keep shtum.'

Oh, dear, Rupert thought, he's not going to like this. Aloud, he said, 'Well, I don't know that anyone's unhappy. But they're not very responsive. I'm sure they listened to the Canon's sermons, and they certainly respected him, but I suppose most of them came to Mass out of a sense of duty. To be honest, Father Dan, I sometimes watched people coming out of church after the service, and it struck me that they didn't look – well, animated, you know. Oh, I've just remembered there is one person who gets a bit disgruntled, Kate Moriarty. Actually, she's really nice usually, and she's been jolly kind to me. She invited me to supper once, but the Canon said ...' he stopped, blushing.

'Don't tell me the Canon said you were not to go?'

'Yes, he did. But it was for good reasons,' he added hastily. 'Kate's husband is a non-Catholic, you see, and ...'

Dan thumped the table. 'Stop!' he told the startled Rupert. 'One thing I feel strongly about is the word "non-Catholic". Please don't use it, Rupert. Don't you see how exclusive it is? How would you like it if someone labelled you a "non-Methodist" or a "non-Anglican"?'

'I never though of it like that,' Rupert said, 'I'm sorry ...'

'And that's another word I'd like to forbid, at least for a while. You say "Sorry" far too often.' He grinned at the discomfited young man. 'Now, I'm intrigued about this Kate Moriarty. Tell me about her.'

'Well, as I said, she's very nice really, but she can be a bit critical. And she got on the Canon's nerves because she asked so many questions.' He lowered is voice. 'And I'm afraid she doesn't believe in hell, and once I heard her criticising the Pope!'

'Good heavens!' Dan exclaimed, 'she sounds positively evil!'

'Oh, no,' Rupert began ...' but then he saw Dan was laughing.

'Oh dear, Rupert,' he said. 'I guess we've both got an awful lot to learn! But tell me, are there any foreigners in the parish?'

'Not many,' said Rupert. 'Actually there are rather a lot of Poles, but they have their own priest and their own Mass.'

'I see,' Dan looked thoughtful. 'What about refugees and asylum seekers?'

'There are quite a lot in the town now, I've heard, but they're mostly non-Cath ...' he gulped. 'Sorry, not Catholics, they're Muslims and such, so we don't get involved with them.'

To Rupert's consternation, Dan simply stared at him for a moment then he thumped the table even louder.

'Are you telling me, Rupert, that just because these people seeking asylum are not Catholics, our parish hasn't any involvement with them?'

'Well, yes, I mean, no, we don't .... sorry!'

There was a pause. Then Dan said 'It's my turn to say sorry, Rupert. I shouldn't vent my anger on you. What I'd very much like to know is, what was *your* role in the parish?'

'My role? Oh, well, I did all the admin for the parish and I did the garden, such as it is.' His face brightened. 'I love gardening!' he said. 'Oh and I prepared the children for First Confession and First Holy Communion, and I checked the collection on Sundays. I was on the Fete Committee at Christmas and I typed and printed the weekly newsletter.'

'Did you write any of it?'

'Oh, no, the Canon ...'

'Did you ever preach?'

'No, the Canon thought ...'

'Did you visit the sick or housebound?'

'No, the Canon was very good ...'

'Have you done any weddings or baptisms or funerals?'

'Well, no ...'

'Don't tell me, the Canon did them all?'

'Yes, yes, he was a wonderful man.'

'It sounds like it,' Dan said, but Rupert couldn't help wondering if his tone was a bit ironic.

'Right, that's enough of an Inquisition for now, Rupert, let's go out and get some fresh air. I'd like to look round the church and then explore a bit of the area. Then, this afternoon you can take me to meet Kate Moriarty and we'll see if she's any ideas about how we could do something to welcome and befriend the asylum seekers in this town.'

To Rupert it seemed a long way to the Moriartys' house, and it involved walking along streets he had never seen before. He felt foolish because St Bon's was his home ground and yet it was Daniel, armed with a street map, who led the way. What made it worse for Rupert was that he could only just keep up with Daniel who was certainly the older by at least twenty years.

At long last, after an hour's walking, he was relieved to see a sign 'Franklin Terrace' and knew that they were almost there. Soon Daniel was striding across an untidy garden to the shabby front door of what must have once been an elegant Victorian house.

Before Daniel could ring the bell, the door was flung open and a girl of about fourteen stood there glaring at him. Then her gaze softened just a little as she recognised Rupert.

'Oh, hello, Father!' she said. 'You'd better go in. I'm just

– well you might as well know, I'm running away from this madhouse. I can't stand it any more!' She heaved what seemed an impossibly heavy rucksack on to her back, flashed them both a cheery grin and strode off down the street.

'Er – oughtn't we to try to stop her?' Rupert asked.

'I don't think so.' Daniel smiled. 'She looks pretty normal to me and I guess she'll be back tomorrow if not before. Come on, let's explore further!'

Inside the house it was warm and there was an appetising smell ahead of them. The place was as shabby inside as it had been on the outside, but the walls were painted in bright colours and various drawings, most of them obviously the work of children, were blu-tacked on to them, next to two or three beautiful watercolours.

It was noisy, bewilderingly noisy. From somewhere upstairs came the thud of loud pop music which conflicted with the soothing sound of classical music being played somewhere ahead. 'Mozart?' whispered Rupert, but Daniel shrugged. 'You tell me, Rupert. I'm tone deaf.' Then he smiled and added 'But I've got a keen sense of smell! Come on, this must be the kitchen.' He pushed open the door ahead and both men went in.

The kitchen was a large airy room, full of activity. Another teenager, long-haired and of indeterminate sex, was playing the piano with considerable flair. At the big table two girls were sitting, absorbed in what was presumably their homework. The older one, who seemed older than the one they had already encountered, struck Rupert as unusual. She had a mop of unruly, bright auburn curls and underneath them a face that seemed strangely serene for someone so young. The little girl was about eight years old. She wore glasses and her hair was neatly tied in plaits. Both, in spite of the noise, were obviously concentrating on their studies. On the floor lay a baby, chuckling and waving his chubby legs in the air. The woman who had been bending over the oven when they entered, stood and seeing Daniel and Rupert, smiled warmly.

'Hi, Father,' she said, holding out her hand to Rupert, and looking at Daniel she added, 'And I expect you're our new priest? Welcome to the chaos!' Daniel liked her on sight.

'We just met your daughter as we were coming in. She looks just like you. Are these all yours too?'

'Well, yes. We're all one family. There's George upstairs in his room. I guess you can hear him! He's been with us since he was thirteen and he's nearly eighteen now. This,' she indicated the others, who looked up briefly as she introduced them, 'is Imogen, our eldest daughter, who is doing her A Levels. Tilly, who's just run away, again, comes next. After Tilly comes Tom, our eldest son; he's about to take his Grade 5 in piano.' Kate walked over to the younger girl and put her arm round her. 'This is Pippa. She's only been with us a few months. Her mother is in hospital. After Tom was born we had a big gap because Robbie, my husband, was away for six years working in the Middle East. He's home now, thank God. Oh, and I nearly forgot, how could I?' She bent down and scooped up the baby. 'This is Barnabas. Isn't he wonderful? But come and sit down, Rupert. Sorry I'm wittering on so. I haven't even asked your name, Father.'

'He's Father Daniel Spring,' Rupert volunteered.

'Well, please sit down, Daniel. We'll have some tea. I've just made some cheese scones and a chocolate cake. But if you could just hold on a moment, I must do something about Tilly. Tom, please will you borrow George's bike and go after her. Talk to her, she'll listen to you.'

Tom stood up and pushed the hair off his face. Grinning at Rupert he snatched a scone from a plate on the table. 'I'm sorry Mum, I can't. I've got my Grade 5 tomorrow and I've just got to revise my theory.'

Kate was pouring the tea and gesturing to the priests to

help themselves to the food. Neither needed to be asked twice. But now Kate was looking worried. 'I'm sorry, Rupert, Daniel,' she said, 'but I'll have to leave you. I can't have Tilly wandering about the streets on her own.'

'Don't worry, you go,' said Dan. He grinned, 'We're very happy here, aren't we Rupert?'

But then Imogen spoke. 'Mum, I'll go,' she said quietly.

'But what about your revision? It's so important ...'

'No,' the girl answered firmly. 'It's more important to get Tilly home. I think she'll listen to me. I'll do my best anyway.' She glanced at the two priests. 'Goodbye, Father,' she said to Rupert, and her rather solemn face broke into a warm smile. 'Goodbye, Father Daniel, and welcome to St Bon's!'

When Imogen had gone, Tom left the piano and Pippa cleared her books away and everyone except Barnabas who had been given a wooden spoon and a saucepan to play with, sat at the table and enjoyed the food.

'Your family must keep you pretty busy, Kate?' Dan commented.

'Yes, they certainly do. Of course I love them and I love being with them, but I was a social worker and I do miss my job. I do quite a bit of voluntary work though. I visit the hospice on Mondays and the prison on Tuesdays. Wednesdays I aim to clean the house, but as you can see, it seldom gets done. On Thursdays I work in an advice centre and on Fridays I go over to Braunton to see my mother. She's wonderful, ninety-three and still looking after herself, but she's getting a bit forgetful. She loves to hear news of the family. Then at weekends we all do things together, Robbie and the children and I. We don't have much money, with the mortgage on this house and Rob being the only earner, but we do have a wonderful life.'

'Yes, I can see that,' Dan said. 'You seem to do such a lot. I expect you can't be much involved in the parish?'

'Look,' said Kate, 'believe it or not, there is a relatively

21

quiet room in this house. Pippa, let me know if Barney needs anything. Come along with me, Rupert and Dan.'

The 'quiet room' was in the front of the house and a fire was laid in the grate. Kate took a box of matches and was about to set fire to the kindling when Dan said, 'Here, let me. I love lighting fires and I'd like to do something useful.'

The priests stayed for an hour. Kate said, 'In answer to your question, Dan, no, I'm sorry we're not much involved in the parish. I had one or two run-ins with the Canon you see. He was very angry when we sent Imogen to the Church of England school. She's strong and heathy now, but as a little girl she had to have an operation on one of her feet, and she couldn't walk very far. It's over a mile to St Bon's school, and St John's, where she went, is just round the corner. I was angry too, and had intended to send the others to the Catholic school but we didn't after that. Then some time later I asked the Canon if we could have a Justice and Peace group in the parish and he said, 'Not if it's run by you, Kate Moriarty, you have caused scandal enough in this parish!'

'But I've done nothing but talk about myself since you arrived. I know Rupert just a bit, but tell me something about you.' She smiled. 'No marks for guessing you're Irish?'

'You're right of course, Kate,' Dan said, 'but the happiest time of my life was spent not in Ireland but in Ecuador.'

Rupert and Kate both listened intently as Dan described his years in South America and his love for the people there. He told them how much they had taught him by their warmth and simplicity and especially by their tremendous capacity for joy and celebration.

'But I thought Ecuador was one of the poorest countries in the world,' Kate said.

'Oh, yes, it is,' Dan agreed, 'almost every family in my parish of thousands went hungry every day, but in spite of everything, they just loved life. It almost broke my heart to leave.'

Kate grinned, 'And now you're landed with St Bon's!' she said. 'I'm afraid we're not so good at joy and celebration. Never mind, Dan, you have Rupert here to support you.'

That night Rupert found it hard to get to sleep. He kept going over the day in his mind, recalling the things this strange priest, who let people call him by his Christian name, had said and done. He felt dazed but not sleepy. In his mind he went over and over again the experience of being in the Moriarty house. He wondered what Dan thought of Kate.

On the way back he had ventured to ask, 'Will you ask Mrs Moriarty to do something about people seeking asylum?'

Dan laughed. 'No,' he said, 'I guess she's already involved with them. But in any case, I think she does more than enough, don't you, Rupert?'

Just before he fell asleep the young priest remembered what Kate had said at the end of their visit. 'Never mind, Dan, you have Rupert here to support you.'

Anxiously, he wondered, was Kate being sarcastic? And he sighed, thinking, maybe life with the Canon was easier, after all. At least, you knew where you were with the Canon!

CHAPTER THREE

Dan and Rupert were two very different people, but as they grew to know each other during Dan's first few weeks at St Bon's, they developed a strong liking and respect for each other. Rupert was a tad apprehensive: he was never sure what Dan would say or do next, and was also afraid of not being able to meet his mentor's expectations. Both men thought of Dan in this role; Rupert had learnt very little in his year with Canon Murphy and had hardly matured in any way.

Occasionally, Dan felt impatient with the young man's lack of confidence, and out of Rupert's hearing would mutter to himself, 'He's a wimp and a wuss!' But he was beginning to feel a real affection for 'the boy' as he called him, and admired his sensitivity and eagerness to do the right thing.

Dan decided, only half reluctantly, that the best way to deal with Rupert's nervousness was to throw him in at the deep end, in other words give him responsibility for something that would be a real challenge. So one evening, when Rupert was washing up after the supper Dan had made (they had a rota for mealtimes, and Dan admitted that Rupert was by far the better cook), Dan told him it was time they shared out the parish work properly.

'I'd like you to tell me which areas you would least like to take on,' Dan began.

'The prison or the youth work?' he said. Rupert didn't hesitate. 'I don't think I'm ready to take on either of those.'

'But will you ever be ready unless you try?' Dan spoke gently.

Rupert shook his head miserably. 'I suppose not' he mumbled.

'Well then, which of those two options would be the harder for you?'

Rupert was beginning to feel panicky. For him, either would be a nightmare.

'I'm not sure, Dan,' he said, 'but if I absolutely had to take one of them on, I'd rather it wasn't the prison, please.'

Dan couldn't help a chuckle. 'Look, Rupert,' he said, 'it can't be as bad as you think. But I believe you should have a stab at one of them. So let's say you make a start on the Youth Club next week. I think they meet on Tuesdays and Fridays.'

Rupert sighed, 'Okay,' he said, 'I will try, but I can't make any promises ...'

Dan interrupted, 'I'm not asking for promises,' he said, 'I'm asking for courage and a little faith in yourself. Think about it and come back to me when you've got some ideas.'

Dan didn't realise that Rupert was literally frightened until he went round to lock up the church that night and found Rupert kneeling in front of the statue of Mary with his head bowed in his hands.

He walked quietly up to the young man, who hadn't heard him come in, and placed a hand on his shoulder. He spoke gently.

'Rupert? What is it? You're not worrying about the young people, are you?'

'Yes, yes, I'm sorry Dan. I know I'm gutless but I also know I'll be no good. I don't know any young people. I don't talk like them, I don't dress like them. They'll see me as silly, out of touch, and I am. They'll laugh at me. I won't know what to say or do! Please don't make me do this!'

Dan looked closely at Rupert and saw that he'd actually been crying. He was also shivering.

'It's freezing in here,' Dan said. ' Come on, let's get you

inside. I've lit a fire and we can have something warm – or something alcoholic – to drink and talk this over.'

Rupert responded to the older man's kindly tone.

'Yes, yes, I'm sorry ...' He got up.

'Sh!' said Dan. 'Don't start saying sorry. Come on, let's get over to the house.' He put his arm across Rupert's shoulder as they walked across from the church. Indoors he directed him to sit close to the fire. He put another couple of logs on the fire and uncorked a bottle of wine. Then, pouring some into a glass he gave it to Rupert, saying, 'I've been too much of a bully. I didn't realise what a big deal this is for you, lad. So let's see if we can work something out.'

'I know I'm a wimp,' Rupert said. 'I'm a coward too. I just can't bear the thought of having to face a group of young people I know nothing about. I won't know what to say, what to do. Honestly, Dan, I'll be useless!'

'Well, how would it be if we got just one of those terrifying youngsters to come round and give you some advice? Somebody already in the club?'

Rupert's face brightened. 'Oh, well, yes, that seems like a good idea.'

'So, do you know any young people in the parish?'

'No,' Rupert admitted, 'not to speak to, that is.'

'You have met one or two who might well be in the Youth Club.'

'Have I?' Rupert was puzzled.

'Yes, those nice kids of Kate Moriarty's. You remember – the girl who was running away, Tilly, I think and the younger one with glasses, Pippa, wasn't it? I can't remember the name of the redhead ...'

'Imogen!' Rupert supplied, then blushed. 'Do you think she's in the Youth Club?'

'I've no idea, Rupert, but would it be too difficult for you to phone and find out?'

Rupert looked at him, wondering if he was being sarcastic, then decided to give him the benefit of the doubt. 'No, that's no problem,' he said, and went out to look up the Moriartys' telephone number.

The following Wednesday evening Rupert opened the door to Imogen. She smiled and he noticed again how her face lit up. She accepted his offer of a cup of coffee and followed him into the kitchen while he made it. She put her cold hands round the mug and said, ' Mm – that's just how I like it.'

Rupert, who had intended to present himself as confident and cool, decided that this girl deserved honesty. 'It's really good of you to come round, Imogen,' he said. She interrupted, 'My friends call me Immo,' she said.

'Oh, well, that's a shame. Imogen is so pretty ...' he felt himself blushing.

'I don't mind, call me what you like. But what shall I call you?'

'Just Rupert,' he said. 'But I asked you round because Father Dan has asked me to lead the Youth Group, and I know it's feeble of me, but frankly, Imogen, I'm terrified. I've no idea what to do or what to say, and I'm plain scared of some of the boys – and girls too. I've seen them in the town centre, especially on a Friday night. Even the words they use, the language ...!'

'I know,' Imogen said. 'I don't like it either. But you soon get used to the odd 'fuck', well, not the 'odd' fuck because they use it all the time – but it means nothing, nothing at all. It's certainly not worth getting het up about.'

'Sorry,' said Rupert. 'I know I do get het up about things. It's my weakness, well, one of my weaknesses.'

Imogen laughed. 'You haven't a very high opinion of yourself have you? And before you say anything, I think that's very nice. It's a change from the brash, pushy young men I come across. But I'd like to ask you something, Rupert. You said Father Dan asked you to lead the Youth Group. Was that how he put it?'

'I'm not sure, I don't remember. Why?'

'Well, we already have a leader. He was elected by the members. I think you would go down better if you took rather a back seat, at least to begin with.' She grinned at his obvious relief.

'Look, Rupert, I mustn't stay any longer. I've got loads of homework to do tonight. But how would it be if I came round again next Wednesday with one or two of the others from the group, so that you can get to know each other a bit, and we can pool our ideas?'

'That would be great, Imogen' he said, 'thank you very, very much. I'm so grateful for your help. I feel a whole lot better about things.'

She was already putting on her coat. She grinned up at him. 'I'll try to persuade a couple of those terrifying lads to come with me, next time!' He opened the door for her and she ran down the path. At the gate she turned and waved. 'Thanks for the excellent coffee!' she called.

Shortly afterwards Dan came in, after visiting a sick parishioner. He took one look at Rupert's face. 'I can see things are looking up!' he said.

CHAPTER FOUR

After three weeks of cooking two meals a day and making a somewhat feeble stab at keeping the house clean on top of all their work in the parish, Dan came to the dispiriting conclusion that it was too much for them. He didn't know how to broach the subject of appointing a housekeeper with Rupert. The young priest had a real gift for cooking; the food he prepared was far more creative and delicious than anything Dan could produce, but he was so lacking in confidence and it seemed cruel to deprive him of the one thing at which he excelled and knew it. In addition, Dan knew how miserable Rupert had been under the ministrations of Mrs McNab, and he feared the very word 'house-keeper' would depress him.

Such thoughts were churning around in his brain one Friday morning while he was making coffee in the kitchen. Rupert was upstairs, hoovering, and didn't hear the door-bell, so Dan went to open the door. The stout, elderly woman standing there looked familiar but Dan didn't know her name. She had a round, weather-beaten face and short grey hair. She was smiling.

'You don' t know me, Father' she said, 'but I'm one of your flock.' She held out her hand. 'I'm Peggy Macdonald.'

Dan welcomed her into the house, but she had hardly sat down when she jumped up and ran towards the kitchen. 'Quick! Something's burning!' she shouted, and then, as she took in what had happened she calmed down.

'I'm sorry, Father' she said, 'I didn't mean to startle you. I thought I smelt burning but it was only the milk boiling over.' Before he could stop her, Peggy took charge of the situation. 'Go and sit down, Father. I'll see to this, and then I'll make a fresh pot of coffee. For you, and Father Rupert, is it?'

'Well, yes, thank you, Peggy. This is very good of you. I'll call Rupert down. Make enough to have a cup yourself.'

Ten minutes later the three of them sat drinking coffee. Dan wished they had bought some biscuits. He looked at Peggy as she joked with Rupert. He liked her cheerful, open face and her rather noisy laugh. 'A comfortable body,' he thought, 'that describes her exactly!'

'You know, I only came for a second,' Peggy said, 'and I don't want to waste your time. I just wanted to ask if it's all right to put this poster up in the church porch.' She rummaged in her capacious bag and pulled out a slightly crumpled roll of paper. Opening it out she showed it to the priests. The paper was white and someone had written in black ink: 'Jumble Sale in St Bon's church hall, Saturday 3rd March 2-4pm. In aid of refugees and people seeking asylum.'

'Oh, that's brilliant!' Dan said. 'I was so much hoping to find someone in the parish who was interested in those poor people.'

'It's very slow,' Peggy said, 'but there's one or two people now who are befriending asylum seekers. It would be good if we could have a party for them where they could do the entertaining. And if one of you could preach about it, that would be wonderful.'

Dan was amazed to hear Rupert's immediate response. 'I will,' he said, 'but I'd need to come and get to know some of them first.'

Peggy stood up. 'Oh, thanks, Father, you've made my day!'

As he walked her to the door, Dan said, 'Do you work, Peggy?'

She grinned and made a rueful face. 'Not any longer!'

she said, 'I was made redundant at the biscuit factory. And where would I get a job at my age? I'm going on sixty.'

Just then Rupert came out of the sitting room office waving Peggy's poster.

'Sorry, Dan,' he said, 'I've just had an idea'. Turning to Peggy he said, 'How many copies of this do you have?'

'Oh, just the one,' she said. 'As you can see, I'm not much good at lettering.'

'Well, I've done a lot of stuff on the computer. How would it be if I re-designed this a bit? I'd keep your words of course. But I could use coloured paper and print it in different colours. I could make lots of copies ...' He stopped suddenly, feeling foolish. 'I'm sorry, Peggy, it was just a silly idea. I got a bit carried away.'

'No, no,' Peggy said. 'Please, if you could do that, I'd be ever so grateful.' She looked at Dan again. 'And thanks for the coffee,' she said. 'Thank *you*,' they chorused, as Dan gently closed the door behind her.

He grinned at the younger man. 'Well, Rupert,' he said, 'you've certainly got your work cut out – a galvanising sermon to preach, and a stunning poster to design!' Then seeing Rupert's all to familiar apologetic look coming over his face, he said sincerely, 'I'm really impressed. Good for you! But before we do anything else, there's another matter I need to consult you about.'

They went back into the sitting room.

'I was wondering what you thought of Peggy?'

Rupert didn't hesitate. 'Oh, she's lovely' he said. 'I really liked her a lot. Didn't you?'

'Yes, I did. I've been wondering about asking your advice.' (He ignored Rupert's raised eyebrows) 'You see, Rupert, I feel all this cooking and housework is too much for us. We're both getting exhausted trying to fit it in on top of visiting and the sacraments, and preaching, and the hospital, and prison ... well, I don't need to go on. Personally I don't like cooking, but you are a dab hand, of course ...'

'You mean you want me to do it all?' Rupert didn't sound exactly enthusiastic.

'No, no, of course not. You work just as hard as I do. No, but I did wonder if you thought it would be a good idea to get someone in to help us?'

Predictably, Rupert looked downcast. 'You mean a housekeeper?' he said.

'No, I don't mean a housekeeper. I mean someone who would come in and cook for us and do the housework and go home again around tea-time. I thought we could perhaps ask Peggy ...'

'Oh, yes! Oh Dan, that's a brilliant idea! Please, I'd be all for it!'

Dan laughed at his eagerness. 'Well, that's all right then. But we'll have to see what the lady herself thinks. I'm tied up for the rest of the day but I could go round and see her tonight.'

Peggy had left her address with Rupert and Dan had no difficulty in finding her house. It was on a small estate of social housing, not far from the centre of Barnham. Peggy answered his knock, and beaming, invited him in. The room was quite small, and no-one could possibly doubt that Peggy was a Roman Catholic. There were holy pictures everywhere, and over the fireplace, in pride of place, a picture of the Sacred Heart.

It was not at all to Dan's taste, but at once it put him in mind of his mother's cottage in County Cork. Her sitting room looked almost exactly like Peggy's but whereas his mother still lived in the house where he was born, surrounded by fields with views of the hills and the sound of the river flowing nearby, Peggy's flat was surrounded in all directions by more houses, and the unbroken rumble of traffic was the only sound outdoors.

As Dan sat down he asked, 'Do you ever see the stars, Peggy?' She looked dumbfounded. 'Well just a bit, sometimes, Father,' she said. 'You can't see much because of the orange light from the street lamps. But I've a sister married to a Yorkshire farmer. They live way out on the moors and I visit sometimes. The night sky is beautiful there.'

She offered Dan tea or coffee, but he said, 'I'm only here for a few minutes, Peggy. I just wanted to ask you to think about something. Rupert and I can't manage the cooking and the cleaning very well, not on top of everything else, and we wondered if you would consider working for us. It would mean coming in every day, say from ten till four, cooking for us and doing the housework too. Rupert went to see the Finance Committee this afternoon, and there would be no problem about paying you a proper wage. But I realise it's a lot to ask, and you'll need to think it over carefully. If you could let us know by the end of the month, and if you say Yes, we can spell out all the details ...'

He stopped, seeing that Peggy had gone red in the face and tears had sprung to her eyes.

'I say yes!' she said. 'I don't need to think it over. It's like a dream come true for me. When can I start?'

'Whoa! Steady on, Peggy,' Dan laughed. 'This is great news for us. But we will have to sort out the details. Could you come round on Saturday? We'll both be there and we can discuss it all.'

He got up to go, and as he turned to say goodbye he suddenly grinned.

'Look, Peggy, young Rupert is a splendid cook. You'll have to let him make supper once in a while – on your day off, perhaps?'

Then he was gone.

CHAPTER FIVE

Wilfrid and Lydia Drew were prominent members of St Boniface's parish, and highly respected in Barnham where Wilfrid was the senior partner in a firm of solicitors. Lydia hadn't worked after her marriage, but she was president of the Catholic Women's League in the parish and leader of the prayer group. On the rare occasions when Canon Murphy had needed to consult a layperson, it was always to Wilfrid that he had turned.

On the first Monday of every month, the Core members of the Prayer Group met at the Drews' house to plan meetings and decide on a speaker they might invite. They all liked coming to Lydia's house, where they met in a large pleasant room with an easy chair for everyone. Norah McGinty did not have a very high opinion of Lydia, but as she walked to the house with Kevin Saunders one Monday evening, she confided in him: 'I've got to admit I like coming, even on a night like this. It's a bit of a luxury for me. And whatever else, Lydia knows how to act the hostess.'

Kevin agreed. 'I don't know where she gets those cakes and biscuits, Norah, and I do appreciate real coffee. You can't deny it, Lydia's a generous woman.'

'Humph!' Norah was hardly convinced. 'It's easy to be generous when you're as rich as the Drews.'

The coffee and cakes were provided at the end of the meeting as Lydia knew that otherwise they would never get started. She was a stickler for punctuality, and it was a source of irritation to her that Sister Julian was nearly always late. This time she arrived a good ten minutes after everyone else, breathless and contrite. 'Oh, I'm so sorry, everybody,' she said, beaming round the group as she pulled off her tatty old jacket. 'I bumped into Nelson on my way here and you know what he's like, he just started on one of his stories and I hadn't the heart to stop him, poor old dear.'

Lydia was not pleased. 'You're a saint, Sister,' she said, 'but you shouldn't be taken in by the likes of Nelson. He's a scrounger, if ever there was one. The dear Canon was quite right not to allow him to sleep in the church, and I'm surprised Father Spring lets him get away with it. He never washes and – oh, but don't let me get started. You all know what I think about Nelson O'Grady.'

No-one responded, some because they wanted to get on with the meeting, others because they were anxious not to upset Lydia by disagreeing with her, Ernest Gage, because he had heard it all before, many times over. So Lydia handed out the meeting's agenda, and with everyone settled and attentive, she began, 'We've got to do something about Kate Moriarty. I know she means well, but she's spoiling the meetings for everyone else!'

There was an awkward silence, then Kevin, who was wondering if he had a vocation for the priesthood, asked, 'How do you mean, Lydia?'

Before Lydia could answer, Sister Julian said, 'There certainly was a difference last time when Kate wasn't with us,' she said, uncertainly.

Then Norah McGinty spoke firmly 'I like Kate', she said.

Lydia sighed. 'We all like Kate,' she said, 'but that's not the point, Norah. She doesn't stick to the rules.'

'I agree with Lydia,' said Ernest Gage who was the parish organist. 'The time before last when I was leading the meeting she really upset me. I was trying to keep up the praise, and wanted us to sing another chorus, but she interrupted with her intercessions and threw me completely.'

Kevin, who was easily the youngest in the prayer group and somewhat in awe of Lydia, nonetheless felt he had to speak up. 'But maybe Kate was right,' he said. 'maybe we should spend more time at the meetings interceding for people. There are so many people and situations in need of prayer.'

'No, no, Kevin,' Lydia said, 'you don't understand. It wasn't the *time* for intercessions. No, someone will have to speak to Kate. It can't go on like this.'

At that moment there was a tap on the door and Wilfrid Drew walked in. Lydia frowned. They had agreed that Wilfrid would never interrupt her meetings. 'What is it?' she asked curtly.

'It's Father Dan. He wants you, Lydia. It sounded urgent.' Lydia sighed and got up. ' Sorry,' she said to the others, 'I'd better take this.' She left the room and walked briskly to the phone. 'Yes, Father,' she said without preliminary. 'What can I do for you?'

'Oh, Lydia, I hope you can help,' Dan said. 'I've got a young girl here, Jenny Bristow. You may know her? No? Well, that doesn't matter. She shared her flat with her older brother Ken, and she's in great distress because he's been killed in an accident. She's only eighteen and I don't think she should be on her own tonight. I know you have plenty of room and Jenny needs a bed for the night, and more importantly she needs comfort and love. I thought of you, Lydia.'

'Oh, Father, I'm sorry,' Lydia said, 'of course I would have had her here, but I'm busy this evening. You of all people will understand. It's the Core members of the Prayer Group's meeting, you see.'

'Yes, I do see,' Dan said. His voice sounded strangely flat. 'Can you suggest anyone else?'

Lydia didn't hesitate. 'Try Kate Moriarty,' she said.

Kate Moriarty had been home half an hour when the phone rang. She had spent a week doing a sponsored walk across the length of the county to raise money for cancer research. It had rained most of the week, and she had been sleeping or trying to sleep on the floor of various village halls. There were blisters on both feet and she was longing for a hot bath and to sleep in her own bed.

Robbie had put young Barnabas to bed and now he was making scrambled eggs for supper. George was, as ever, playing his music in the attic; Tom, Tilly and Pippa had all gone to a friend's birthday party and Imogen was laying the table.

Kate was in the sitting room with Madge from two doors away talking about her marital problems when they heard the telephone.

'Can you get it, love?' Robbie called. 'I'm just at a crucial stage with the eggs.' Kate laughed, thinking what a perfectionist he was. She excused herself to Madge and hurried to the phone. She listened to what Dan had to say.

'Yes, Dan,' she said. 'Yes, of course we'll have Jenny here. The poor kid, how absolutely wretched for her.' Dan spoke again. 'Sure,' she said, 'sure it's no trouble. Bring her round right away.'

CHAPTER SIX

It was Wednesday evening, a fine night with a full moon, as Imogen walked towards the presbytery with Basher Ross and Cody Shuttleworth. They were the only two she had managed to persuade to come along. She was fervently hoping they wouldn't be too much of a shock for Rupert.

Basher was huge and very black. He was six foot five inches tall with dreadlocks and tattoos on every available part of his anatomy, most of which was mercifully concealed. He wore one plastic earring in the shape of a naked girl and several heavy chains with medallions adorned his massive chest. His jeans had tattered ends, his trainers were badly scuffed, but his teeth were white and even and the skin of his face was unblemished.

Cody's head reached Basher's waist. She was a tiny girl and looked painfully thin. She wore a mini skirt the size of a pocket handkerchief and a top that was barely decent. She had a small white face and very heavy eye makeup, but the most noticeable thing about Cody was her hair. It was styled in tufts of orange, green and blue. And Cody wore scent.

'Phew!' said Basher, 'you stink, Cody Shuttleworth! That's a disgusting smell you got on yer.' Cody only smiled. 'Tell us about this priest then, Immo' she said, ignoring Basher.

'Yeah, what's 'is name then?'

'Rupert. His name's Rupert.'

'What! You're kiddin'!' said Basher. ' What sort of name is that? Rupert! Huh! You're jokin', please tell me you're jokin'!'

'No, I'm not.' Imogen said firmly. 'There's nothing wrong with the name.'

'Yeah, it's better than Basher, any day!' said Cody.

They were turning into Rupert's street and Imogen found herself feeling nervous. She stopped, and the others looked at her.

'Look, Basher, Cody. I want you to promise me something, please!'

'What?' Basher growled suspiciously.

'I want you to promise me that just for the time we're with Rupert, you won't use the 'f' word or the 's' word or any of the words you know perfectly well are offensive to some people.'

'And if we do this for you?' Basher challenged her.

Imogen was caught off guard. 'Well, what would you like me to do?'

Basher grinned. 'I'd love you to come out with me, Immo,' he said.

Imogen hesitated only a fraction of a second. 'Okay!' she said, 'I'd really like that, Basher. I'll come out with you, just once. Mind you, I'll be watching and listening to you very carefully, and if there's as much as a hint of a swear word, I'll change my mind.' 'Don't worry about me, Immo,' said Cody, 'I won't let you down.'

Imogen looked at her and suddenly realised what a pathetic little ceature she was under all the bravado of false glamour.

'Thanks, Cody,' she said. 'I know I can count on you.'

In the end it wasn't nearly as difficult as both Imogen and Rupert had anticipated. Each of the four of them made a tremendous effort in self-control. When he first saw them Rupert wanted to run away and hide and it was only the gentle serenity of Imogen (as he perceived it, since she in fact had never felt more tense) that made him go through the introductions and then lead them into the sitting room.

In the weeks since Dan's arrival, the sitting room had

been transformed. It was warm and inviting and Rupert had made some custard tarts and fruit scones, both still warm from the oven.

'Jesus, man!' said Basher sniffing appreciatively, striding over towards the food. Imogen felt irritated with herself. I should have included 'Jesus' and 'God' she thought. But Rupert didn't seem to have noticed.

'Here,' he said to Cody, handing her a plate and a napkin and then offering her a scone or a tart. He did the same for Basher who took a handful of each and blew his nose on the napkin.

'These are really ace,' said Cody.

'Yeah, you're cool, man,' Basher echoed, standing up to go for another scone. 'Thanks.'

Imogen was touched by Rupert's ability to stay courteous in the face of the complete lack of manners Basher was showing. She remained anxious throughout the interview, but the other three were now relaxed.

Funny little Cody had the most and the best ideas for how the Youth Club could be improved. Rupert listened and made notes. Basher said little, partly because he was still eating. But in the end Basher it was who came out with words of wisdom which Rupert took to heart.

'Look, Rupe,' he said, 'It will be cool having you in the club, but you want to take it easy, man, at least in the beginning. It's what they call a low profile, see? 'Cos some of them guys is a bit ignorant and they're not used to an oddball like you – no offence, mate.'

After they'd left, Rupert went back into the sitting room and clapping his hands, jumped into the air, uncharacteristically exuberant. 'Yes!' he shouted. Then he noticed Dan who had come in from the kitchen and was scoffing the last of the scones. Rupert felt himself blushing and Dan grinned. 'I take it the meeting went well,' he said.

'Oh yes,' Rupert agreed, 'but it was all down to Imogen. She's wonderful. She's so kind, and calm, and wonderful ...'

He stopped, blushing again. Dan merely raised an eye-brow, but he felt a tiny qualm.

Imogen was happy. She couldn't believe how well it had all gone. At home, she went into the kitchen where her mother was ironing.

'Well, did it go all right?' Kate asked.

'Oh yes, I couldn't have believed how well we all got on. But it was all down to Rupert really. He's wonderful. He's so kind, and gentle and wonderful ...' She stopped, aware that she was blushing.

Kate merely raised an eyebrow and carried on with her ironing, but she was aware of a tiny qualm.

CHAPTER SEVEN

Dan was surprised at how quickly he and Rupert settled into a happy routine, though he realised that Peggy's presence in the house made a huge difference. He also saw that in spite of their differences in age, personality and background, Rupert and he had a lot in common: both loved their work and approached it with enthusiasm and commitment.

There were undoubtedly areas where Rupert was nervous of adventuring, such as the prison, but he had faced up to the challenge of the Youth Club and now actually enjoyed going there. He was a great asset when it came to liturgy, full of creative ideas involving different kinds of worship to suit different people, and he had found ingenious ways of brightening up the rather sombre old church. Naturally, some parishioners, particularly genteel women like Amanda Trumpington and Lydia Drew, preferred Rupert, while the robust no-nonsense men of the parish found Dan more congenial. But as the people saw how well the two priests got on together, such distinctions mattered less.

Rupert admired Dan's easy manner with every sort of person, and at first he was astonished at the number of people he knew personally and the amount of visiting he took on. Without realising it, he began to follow Dan's example and, as his confidence increased, he began to make more and more good friends in the parish. Also unconsciously, Dan learnt from Rupert's gentle courtesy. He began to curb his occasional blunt gruffness when faced with people or situations that angered him. Probably the thing most parishioners noticed about the two men was their friendliness and untiring commitment to hard work.

After Rupert had been with Dan for six months, his parents, Miles and Hester Brownlow came to stay at the presbytery for a few days. Dan thought they looked rather like brother and sister, with silvery hair, mild gentle faces and rather faded blue eyes. The visit went very well. One evening when Rupert had taken his father down to his favourite pub where he knew a number of the locals, Hester was helping Dan prepare the supper. She said, 'We'll always be grateful to you, Dan.'

'Why?' Dan was surprised.

'Rupert's changed so much in the past few months. In his first year, when he was with the Canon, we used to be concerned about him. He did his best not to worry us and to sound cheerful on his weekly telephone call, but we could tell he wasn't really happy. Then someone sent us a photo of him with the Canon. It had been taken by the local press on some occasion or other. We were shocked to see how thin and drawn Rupert looked, and somehow cowed. But now, you have only to look at him! He's filled out, he looks confident and I can see he's really happy. It's as though he is at peace with himself and it's wonderful for Miles to see him like this. We both feel it's all down to you, Dan, and we're deeply indebted to you.'

Dan was embarrassed.

'No, no, you've got it all wrong, Hester,' he said. 'If anything, it's the other way round. Rupert's really good for me. He's knocked off some of my rough edges. I'm only a simple old Irishman, you know, and I've learned to behave with more courtesy and consideration from your son.'

Meanwhile, at the White Hart, Rupert said to his father, 'You know, Dad, I owe you a big apology. I hardly considered your feelings, or Mother's for that matter, when I suddenly announced my conversion to Catholicism. I know it isn't an excuse, but at seventeen I was too preoccupied with myself, with my own concerns and ambitions, to think about how about my words and actions might affect others. I've been wanting to say this for months, but I felt I should do it face to face. Was it a huge shock when I converted? Were you bitterly disappointed?'

Miles smiled across at his son. 'No, no, of course not. It was a surprise, yes, but not a shock, and it was good to see you so focused, especially after Paul.'

Paul was Rupert's older brother, who had dropped out of university and left home to live in a squat.

'How is he?' Rupert asked. 'Does he keep in touch?'

'Occasionally,' Miles smiled, 'usually when he wants money, but not always. He did remember a card for Mothering Sunday and even sent me a card on my birthday ...' He stopped. 'Oh, sorry, Rupert, I'm not getting at you. I can see your life is so full and busy ...'

But Rupert was contrite. 'Dad, I'm really sorry. You see, I'm still so selfish. I'll make a real effort from now on. When is Mother's birthday, I can't exactly remember?'

Miles laughed. 'Actually it's tomorrow,' he said. 'She didn't want me to bring it up, but as you asked me directly ...'

'Dad,' Rupert said, standing up, 'can we go back to the presbytery now? The decent card shops will be closed, but I think I've got time to make something on the computer.'

They hurried back and Rupert disappeared to his room for half an hour. Later, when his parents had gone to bed, he told Dan about the birthday.

'That's great!' Dan said, 'We must organise a celebration. I'll phone Peggy and see if she can come in early enough to make a cake, and we can push the boat out for once. Does Hester like fillet steak?'

'Er, it's not something we usually eat at home, Dan, but I've never known her not like any food. But I have to warn you, she'll hate a big fuss.'

'Let's not make one, then,' Dan said, 'we'll have the meal in the dining room tomorrow night. It's a pity never to use it now that it's so warm and cheerful. And if it's all right with you, we'll ask Peggy to stay for the meal, so your mother isn't so outnumbered. But we won't even mention the birthday until Peg brings in the cake. Then you can sing 'Happy birthday' if you like, as long as you don't ask me to join in – that would ruin it. But that's only my suggestion. What do you think, Rupert? Maybe you would prefer to go out somewhere with your parents, just the three of you?'

'No, no, Dan, that sounds perfect. Thank you.'

Next morning, after he had breakfasted, Rupert took two mugs of tea and the card to his parents. He had made the card on the computer but had written a personal message inside. Hester concealed her surprise and expressed her delight.

'It's my day off,' said Rupert. 'Dan says I can take the car so we could drive out into the country and go for a walk, if you'd like that?'

They arrived back about six o'clock, tired, happy, a little sunburnt and a bit sweaty.

'I wonder if I should change,' mused Hester. 'It's all so relaxed and informal here I don't suppose I need bother. I'll just have a good wash.' She made for the stairs.

'Wait, Mother, it might be a good idea to change. I'm going to, because Dan thought it would be nice to use the dining room tonight. We've never used it before, but now it's decorated it's a really nice room, so it might be appropriate to dress-up – just a little bit.'

'Oh, I didn't realise. Of course I'll change. I'll have a shower too, and might even powder my nose!'

Hester suspected nothing until the moment when Peggy walked in carrying a large cake with pink icing and a great many candles. Rupert struck the first note of 'Happy Birthday' and Peggy and Miles joined in.

'I feel like a child,' said Hester, 'a happy, excited child!'

When the Brownlows left next day, and were waiting

for Rupert to drive them to the station, Dan had a moment with them alone. They shook hands warmly and then Dan said, 'I've been meaning to say this ever since you arrived: I can't help envying you, having a son like Rupert.'

CHAPTER EIGHT

One Sunday morning after Mass, Wilfrid Drew approached Dan and said, 'Could I have a word with you sometime, Father?'

'Sure, Wilfrid, come round to the presbytery now, if it suits you. Rupert will have left the coffee ready. It's his turn to go down for coffee with the parish, but no doubt he will have left some of his special fruit cake. Since we've had Peggy with us he hasn't made many meals, but he's gone in for baking in a big way.'

Once they were in the house, Wilfrid came straight to the point. 'I think we ought to have a Parish Council, Father,' he said, 'to take some of the load off you and Father Rupert.' 'Well, I've been thinking along the same lines, Wilfrid. How would you see us going about it?'

'Well, Father, I assume you will appoint a few of us, people who are reliable and responsible, of course. I think we should have one or two women on it – you have to be careful – I could name at least one feminist in our parish, though I certainly wouldn't want her on the council.' Both men had a picture of Kate Moriarty in their minds but they forbore to mention her.

'I see,' Dan said, 'that would be one way of doing it but I would prefer to go about it differently. I suggest we get some nominations from the people and then everyone can have a vote.'

'Oh, yes, well, I see what you mean, Father. That would certainly be more democratic. Would you like to me organise it? I could explain it all in the newsletter and set a deadline for voting and so on. Shall I do that?'

'Yes, that's very good of you, Wilfrid. I'm afraid I'd have gone on putting it off if you hadn't given me a nudge, so I'm most grateful.'

As he was leaving, Wilfrid turned back to Dan. 'You will be on the council yourself, won't you, Father?'

'Absolutely not!', said Dan.

Wilfrid was known for his efficiency. On the following Sunday, there was an item in the parish newsletter entitled 'Election to St Boniface's Parish Council.'

A clear explanation followed, and those who were interested went home knowing what to do. There were to be six people on the parish council, and nominations were to be handed in by the end of the month. To Dan's disappointment, there were only seven nominations: Wilfrid Drew, William O'Connor, Hilary Clough, Kevin Saunders, George Moriarty, Norah McGinty, Ernest Gage and Nancy Slater.

But Dan seemed pleased when Wilfrid showed him the list.

'It's a really good cross-section,' he said, 'three women and four men, William to speak for the elderly and George for the youth. But it's a real shame there are only six places for seven people,' he added.

'Yes, I know, Father.'

'Couldn't you change it? Couldn't you make it seven places after all?'

Wilfrid was dismayed at the suggestion.

'No, no, Father,' he said. 'You can't mess about with things like that. It would be a sure sign of incompetence. But I tell you what we can do. We can co-opt the person who isn't elected, whenever it's appropriate. I don't suppose they'll mind much.'

The votes were counted in the presbytery two weeks later. Dan, Rupert, Wilfrid and Peggy (at Dan's suggestion) were present. The results were as follows, in order of the number of votes received: 1: Hilary Clough, 2: Ben Shaw, 3: Kevin Saunders, 4: George Moriarty, 5: Norah McGinty, 6: Nancy Slater, 7: Wilfrid Drew.

Wilfred made a supreme effort to hide his feelings, but he failed. Both priests were silent; neither could think what to say. Peggy came to the rescue. 'Oh, bad luck, Wilfrid,' she said, 'and after you've organised it so well. But look, you have only one vote less than Nancy Slater. It was a very close thing.' She turned to Dan. 'Shall I bring some drinks?'

'Yes, please, Peg,' said Dan.

But Wilfrid looked stricken. 'After all I've done for this parish,' he said, 'and that's all the gratitude I get. Why, I've never even heard of Nancy Slater. Won't be staying for a drink, thank you, Father, and by the way, if anyone wants to co-opt me, they can go to hell!' No-one was surprised when he slammed the door.

'Oh, dear,' said Peggy, 'poor man. He must feel such a fool. And tomorrow, he'll feel even worse, for taking it so badly in front of us.'

'You're right, of course, Peg,' said Dan, 'and Wilfrid's a good man. But just a bit ...' he hesitated.

'Officious?' Rupert supplied

'Yes, that's the word. And he puts people's backs up. To be honest, he puts mine up sometimes. He's not a popular man. But I blame myself. I should have realised it might happen.'

'Nonsense!' Peggy exclaimed. 'I tell you what, Father, how would it be if, in say a month's time, I cooked a nice dinner and you invited Wilfrid and Lydia? I think they'd like that.'

'I'm sure they would. What a good idea, Peg. What would we do without her?' he asked Rupert.

'I think we'd collapse entirely, Dan. Shouldn't we say we will do this on one condition, that Peggy joins us for the meal?'

'No!' Peggy was emphatic. 'It's kind of you, but our Wilfrid's a bit of a snob and poor Lydia's worse. It would completely spoil it for them if they had to eat with a servant.' 'I'm afraid you're right, Peg,' said Dan, 'but we still haven't opened that bottle. At least join us for a drink!'

The following week Amanda Trumpington made a rare visit to the presbytery. Dan saw her coming from his office window and pulled a face. 'Rupert,' he called. 'Amanda T. is coming. Please would you deal with her? She's more your sort than mine.'

'Thanks a bunch!' said Rupert, who was slowly getting the confidence to be cheeky.

Amanda was already ringing the door bell. Dan quickly slipped into the kitchen as Rupert invited her in. She was a tall woman, impeccably groomed and dressed, and Rupert felt embarrassed to be wearing a scruffy jumper.

'Is Father Dan in?' she asked.

'I'm sorry, he's not here at the moment, Mrs Trumpington'. He told himself that wasn't exactly a lie. 'But do come and sit down. Can I get you something to drink?'

She smiled graciously. 'No,thank you, Father,' she said, 'But I may as well tell you as Father Spring isn't here. I'm the bearer of bad tidings, I'm afraid.'

'Oh, dear, what's happened?'

'It's poor Hilary. Hilary Clough. You will know her, I expect?'

'Yes, of course.' Hilary was one of his favourite parishioners, gentle and wise and strong and about the same age as his mother.

'Well,' said Amanda, 'I'm very sorry to tell you that she has been diagnosed with cancer.'

'Oh, what a shock!'

'Yes, we're all frightfully shocked. She's such a wonderful person. It couldn't happen to anyone nicer. She's been a good friend to me. I shall miss her dreadfully if ...' Amanda was dabbing her eyes with a tissue.

'Oh, please don't say that,' Rupert began. 'Surely they will be able to cure it, cut it out ...' Rupert floundered, not certain what the doctors would actually do.

'Well, I hope so. But I thought I ought to tell Father Spring at once especially as Hilary is on the parish council.'

'Oh, yes,' said Rupert, 'I'd forgotten that. But don't worry about it, and tell Hilary not to worry either. I'm sure Father Dan would say it's a minor matter and we'll soon be able to replace Hilary.'

Amanda stood up suddenly. 'What do you mean, replace her? Nobody could ever replace Hilary, not in my life. You don't know what you're talking about, young man!' As she swept by him Rupert tried to catch her arm. 'But I didn't mean, I only meant ...' Amanda was already out of the door.

Rupert went to tell Dan. 'I've handled it really badly' he said apologetically. Dan smiled. 'At least you didn't say "sorry",' he said, 'but what is it? What's happened?' Rupert told him. 'I'll go round to see Hilary right away' Dan said.

CHAPTER NINE

It was March. The idea for the picnic was hatched by Rupert and Cody. She was fascinated by the young priest; she had never met anyone like him. At the end of one of the Youth Club's meetings she came over to where Rupert was sitting.

'Tell me about how you grew up,' she said.

Rupert was surprised at the question. He still hadn't realised how different he seemed to the young people who were becoming his friends.

'Well, I grew up in a village,' he began. 'My father was …'

'Tell me about the village. What was it like?'

'Well, it was very small and very old. The houses were all built of stone …'

'Was there any thatched cottages? I've seen them on telly. They look so cute.'

'No, some of the cottages may have been thatched at one time. The vicarage where we live is a beautiful house, over three hundred years old, but it has high ceilings and no central heating, so it's bitterly cold in winter.'

'Is the village all by itself? I mean, is it joined on to a town like Barnham?' Cody was trying to picture it.

'No, it's surrounded by fields.'

'Isn't it lonely?'

'No, no, not in the least! You see everybody knows everybody. In some ways we're like a big family, I suppose.'

'Is everybody posh like you?'

Rupert laughed, embarrassed. 'No, Cody, it's like everywhere else, a great mix of characters. And our family isn't posh. My father is the vicar, a Church of England priest. He has to look after five other villages, but we happen to live in Appledown.'

'Appledown! That's a cute name.' Cody said, 'Tell me some more. What grows in the fields?'

Rupert was puzzled. Was Cody having him on? Could she really be so ignorant? 'Well, grass of course. There isn't much arable – that means crops for food. It's mostly stock, you know, cattle and sheep.'

'I've never seen a cow,' said Cody. 'Well, I have in pictures or on telly, but I've never seen a real one. Are they scary?'

Rupert was astonished. 'You're not serious?' he said.

'Course I am. I've never been out of Barnham, except once on a school trip down the motorway to London. But we didn't see no cows.'

'Cody, you've got to be joking?'

'No, honest, Rupert. I swear on my Mum's grave, I ain't never seen a cow.'

Rupert wondered if he shouldn't ask about her mother, but people were waiting to lock up the hall. Another time, he thought.

'I say, Cody, why don't we try and organise a picnic for the Youth Club? We could all go out into the country, where there are plenty of cows and other things to see. Let's put it to the others next time. We could go in May, perhaps, when it's likely to be warmer …'

'Could we?' he was surprised at Cody's excitement. 'Could we really? Oh, I'd love that!'

Imogen and some of the others were a bit doubtful about the picnic. 'Can you guarantee it won't rain, Rupe?' Basher asked. 'I know you got a direct line to him up there, but in my experience, he has been known to say No, in it?'

Rupert wisely decided this was not the time for religious instruction.

'No, of course I have no control over the weather, Basher. But I think it would be worth taking a risk.'

'Yes, I agree,' Imogen said, 'but we have to think about the cost and transport. Not many of us has much money, and nobody has a car. I don't want to put a damper on things. I think it's a lovely idea, Rupert. But we have to be practical, don't we?'

'Yes, of course,' Rupert agreed, encouraged by her praise. 'Look, if you'll leave it with me, I'll see what I can come up with. There may be ways round these problems.'

Rupert was surprised to find he had some organisational skills. He discussed the picnic and its problems with Dan and Peggy. Dan promised he could use the parish car, which held five, at a pinch, and Peggy said she knew a minibus driver who might be willing to drive some of the young people at a cut rate.

'He owes me one,' she said with a grin, 'well, more than one as it happens!' She didn't enlighten the priests any further. The date was fixed for the seventh of May, a list of those who wanted to come drawn up, the minibus organised, people asked to bring sandwiches and drinks, sun cream optimistically advised.

As Rupert was leaving the house on the seventh, Peggy arrived.

'Hello, Peg, you're very early!' Rupert greeted her.

'Well, I wanted to give you some things,' she said. 'I baked them last night. They're not up to your standard, of course, but the kids are bound to get hungry by the end of the afternoon ...' She handed Rupert a large bag. 'It's just buns and biscuits,' she said. Rupert took the bag and thanked her warmly. 'There must be several dozen in here,' he said.

'I've got a little contribution too,' Dan said, emerging from the kitchen where he had been eating his breakfast. 'On a day like this the kids will be wanting ice cream. There's a place in Larkford where they make it and it's delicious. You did say you'll be based in Larkford, didn't you?'

'Yes, the minibus is dropping us there. Then we only have to walk a short way down to the river, and I've got permission from the farmer to use his field.'

'Well, I think this should cover twenty ice creams,' Dan said, handing Rupert a handful of notes. 'You're certainly blessed with the weather and I hope they all enjoy it. Be sure to take a photo of Cody's first encounter with a cow!'

They set off at nine o'clock. Rupert drove the parish car ahead of the minibus. He had four passengers, Basher in the front and three girls in the back. Rupert had rather hoped Imogen would be one of them, but she was in the minibus. The driver struck Rupert as a very pleasant, friendly man, and he reflected again on how much he owed Peggy.

It was a warm sunny day and when they left Larkford they found the meadows full of wild flowers. They saw some cows almost immediately, placid black and white creatures munching away in apparent contentment.

Rupert turned to the group. 'I'm going to take Cody to meet a cow,' he said. ' Is there anyone else who hasn't seen one before?'

One of the smaller boys held up his hand. 'Only on telly,' he said.

'Come on, then,' said Rupert. He took Cody's hand and with the boy trailing nervously behind them they crossed over to the cows. As they got close Cody stiffened, and the boy, Glen, muttered, 'They're big! I'm scared!'

'There's nothing to be scared of,' Rupert assured him. The cows ignored them and went on munching. Then the nearest one lifted its head and looked straight at them. Glen jumped back but Cody stood her ground. 'Gosh, she's beautiful,' she said. 'Now, can we find some sheep?' 'Wait till I've taken your photo,' Rupert said.

The field they were allowed to use sloped down to the

river. It was shallow and wide at this point, and there were several big rocks. To Rupert's relief he didn't need to organise anything. He stayed close to the water just in case there was an accident, and watched the young people enjoy themselves in different ways. Some played ball games, some wrestled, others raced each other across the field. The river was popular for paddling, dodging across the rocks and skimming stones. Cody wanted to pick flowers and Imogen had to explain why this wasn't a good idea.

At around noon Rupert suggested it was time to eat and everyone crowded onto the riverbank and opened their packed lunch. It was Basher who noticed that Glen wasn't eating.

'Where's your sarnies, then?' he asked. Glen blushed. 'I'm stupid,' he said, 'I forgot them.'

Immediately Basher gave him a sandwich and a banana. Then a girl called Susie gave him a chocolate bar, and two or three others reached across offering Glen a share of their food.

'No, no, thanks!' Glen said. 'Look, now I've got more than anybody else!'

Rupert, watching all of this, felt a lump in his throat. 'They're good kids,' he thought, and suddenly remembered the feeding of the five thousand. Maybe it wasn't a miracle, he thought, maybe it was more like this.

After lunch people were sleepy. Most of them sat on the bank, chatting and several of the girls lay down to sunbathe. Imogen came over and sat next to Rupert.

'This was a good idea,' she said. 'It's been brilliant. They're all loving it. It's all thanks to you, Rupert.'

Rupert was pleased but embarrassed. 'Actually it was Cody who gave me the idea,' he said.

They were due to rejoin the minibus at four o'clock. Susie, who had actually been asleep, rolled over. 'What time is it?' she asked. Imogen answered, 'It's nearly three o'clock.'

'Look,' said Susie, 'let's not waste time just lying here. I feel like some exercise.' 'Good idea,' said Imogen, getting up. 'What shall we do? Explore? Go for a walk along the river?'

Most of the girls were standing now. 'I know,' said one. 'Let's do some handstands and cartwheels!'

Susie and Cody were enthusiastic. They both excelled at PE in school and they began to show off, turning expert cartwheels in the grass.

'Come on, Immo, it's easy!' Cody said.

Imogen hesitated. She knew she was fit but she hadn't turned a cartwheel for years. Had she still got the knack?

'Chicken!' one of the boys called.

Imogen laughed. 'Okay, I'll try,' she said, 'but I'm not sure if I can do it.'

To her surprise, she turned a perfect cartwheel and people clapped. 'You're good, Immo!' shouted Basher. 'Let's see you do another.'

Imogen put her hands on the ground and lifted her legs into the air but then one of her hands slipped and she fell with a thud to the ground. Somehow one foot got twisted and crushed under the weight of her body. Rupert jumped up and began running towards her. He looked down and saw her face grimaced in pain, and that instant realised with a shock of terror and delight that he was in love.

'Basher, we've got to carry her to the car,' he said. 'Come on, we mustn't lose any time. The rest of you, please follow us to the village. Cody, it's down to you to see nobody's left behind. I'll take Imogen straight to the hospital. The rest of you who came in the car will have to squeeze into the minibus somehow.'

It was hard, heavy work carrying Imogen, but Basher was steady and careful. They went as fast as they could and the rest of the party straggled behind. As soon as they got to Larkford they settled Imogen into the car and Rupert gave Basher his wallet.

'That's to pay for ice creams for everybody,' he said, 'and I want you to settle up with the minibus driver, please. Here's my mobile number if you need it. Thanks, Basher.'

Then Rupert broke the speed limit.

CHAPTER TEN

However, in the emergency ward, they had to wait for over an hour before Imogen was seen. She sat very still, trying not to make a fuss, but she couldn't help grimacing from the intense pain and once or twice, Rupert saw a tear slide down her cheek. They didn't talk. She didn't feel up to it and he was immersed in troubled thoughts.

'I just can't be in love,' he told himself. 'It's totally inappropriate: she's a schoolgirl and I'm a priest. I've given up my whole life to God and it's impossible. I love God, but I love Imogen too – she's so sweet and warm and vulnerable … Oh, God!' It was a fervent prayer but there were no answers for him. The same thoughts tumbled over and over in his head.

'My Mum …' Imogen suddenly spoke. 'Could you call her, please?' She gave him Kate's number. 'I'm sorry!' said Rupert, 'How stupid of me. I should have thought of that straightaway.' He dialled Kate's number and she walked into the ward fifteen minutes later. 'I took a taxi,' she said. 'Robbie's away with the car. Oh Imogen, my poor love, you look awful. How did it happen?' The sympathy was too much for Imogen and she burst into tears, but then her name was called and she managed to hobble over across to the emergency nurse practitioner.

Things moved faster now. Imogen was given painkillers and x-rayed and diagnosed with a badly sprained ankle. 'You won't be walking for a week or two, young lady,' said the doctor, 'but you're young and healthy so I expect it will heal fairly quickly.'

Rupert drove the two women home and as soon as he

turned to go back to the presbytery his troubled thoughts assailed him again.

Basher was waiting for him outside the front door. 'How's Immo?' he asked. Rupert reassured him and Basher handed him his wallet. 'There's a receipt for the ice cream,' he said, 'and the bus driver wouldn't take nothing. 'E said 'is Mam would tan 'is 'ide if 'e as much as charged a penny. Is that cool or what, man?'

Bewildered, Rupert thanked Basher who said, 'It was a wicked day, Rupe, everybody said so. Thanks. And don't worry about old Immo. She's a tough kid!'

'Kid!' thought Rupert miserably. 'She's probably younger than Basher! What am I thinking of?'

He made up his mind not to see Imogen, not ever again if he could help it. And he decided not to confide his feelings to anyone. It was his dilemma, and he would deal with it. And as soon as Imogen was well, he would give up the Youth Club.

He went upstairs and washed and realised these firm resolutions helped a little, just a very little. At least he was ready to face Dan.But when he went down to the sitting room Dan said, 'Why, Rupert, what ever's the matter? You look dreadful. Was the picnic a disaster?'

'No, no, it was splendid and I'm fine. I'm probably a bit tired because Imogen Moriarty had a fall and sprained her ankle and so Basher and I had to carry her from the picnic field to the car.'

'Oh, dear, the poor child!' Dan exclaimed.

Inwardly, Rupert shuddered. Child, he thought, yes, she's just a child! Aloud he said, 'She's fairly comfortable now. It's just a nasty sprain. Kate came to the hospital and I drove them home afterwards.'

'Good,' said Dan, 'You seem to have done everything right. But what about the youngsters who travelled to Larkford in your car? How did they get back?'

'To be honest, I'm not sure,' Rupert, who had hardly

given a thought to to this, admitted. 'But the bus driver must have brought them back, or Basher would have said. He seemed a decent sort of man.'

'Decent or not, he might have had to break the law by taking more passengers.'

'I'm afraid I didn't think about that, but there's something odd about that driver. He wouldn't take any money. He said his mother would tan his hide if he took any at all! What can that mean?'

Dan was quiet for a moment. Then he said, 'I think it means that Peggy works nearly all day and nearly every day to make our lives as pleasant and as comfortable as possible, and we – or perhaps I should say I – haven't even bothered to find out anything about her personal life.

After breakfast next morning Dan said, 'Will you be going round to the Moriartys' to see how Imogen is?'

'No, not today, Dan,' Rupert said, hoping he was not blushing.

'But I thought it was your day off?'

'Well, yes, but somehow I've got loads to do. I don't think I can fit it in.'

'Righto, I'll go round myself. I like going there. You never know what to expect.'

Glumly, Rupert watched Dan set off. Then he remembered what Dan had said the previous night and went into the kitchen. Peggy was peeling potatoes.

'Peggy, would you mind breaking off for a minute? I'd like to have a word with you. Come into the other room and I'll make some coffee.'

Peggy put down her peeler. 'Bless the lad,' she thought, 'I hope this doesn't take too long.'

When they were both sitting, Rupert began.

'I don't want to pry into your life Peggy, but do you mind telling me what your connection is to the minibus driver we used yesterday?'

'Oh, the silly boy!' was Peggy's response. 'I told him to

give away nothing but he could never keep a secret! Well, you might as well know, he's my son, Walter. He's a good lad really, only he doesn't always listen.'

'We all thought he was very nice,' Rupert assured her, 'too nice, actually. Apparently he wouldn't accept any money for the fare!'

'Well, he's built up a very good little business there. It's his own minibus and he does work very hard. But I'm not having any son of mine making money out of folk as are as good as Father Dan and you. I told him, "It's not on" and he agreed, no problem. What are friends for, anyway?'

'Yes, Peggy but in a way that's the point. Dan explained to me last night that we've never made an effort, either of us, to learn about your personal life, your history, your problems, so in a way, we are not very good friends to you, and we're really sorry.'

'I've just had an ordinary life. It's not really interesting. And anyway you're both so busy trying to solve other people's problems it's better that you don't have to concern yourselves with mine. Not that I have any problems now, anyway.'

'Well, that's good,' Rupert said. 'But tell me, is Walter your only son?'

'Yes, he's my only child now. When I found I was pregnant with him I married his father, Jack Macdonald. Then Jack died from an accident in the factory, just two months before our little girl was born. I called her Jacqueline after him, but she died before she was a year old. So it was just Walter and me, and I went to work in the biscuit factory. I didn't like it much, but I had some good mates there and the wages meant that Walter and me were all right. We had a holiday once, we went to Scarborough. Walter loved it.'

'Is Walter married?'

'Oh, yes, he's got a wife, Shirley, the best daughter-in-law you could wish for, and they have twins, Maudie and Jackie. Maudie was after Shirley's mother, and Jackie after her auntie that died as a baby. Shirley is a dinner lady at the school where the twins go.'

'Are they Catholics?' ventured Rupert.

'Oh, bless you no. They were married in the Methodist chapel but they don't go to church or chapel now. Still, I'm not biased when I say that they're good people.'

'No, I'm sure you're not, Peggy. And it must be great to have your family so near.'

'Yes, it certainly is,' agreed Peggy.

Just then he heard the key in the door and Dan came in. 'Oh, I thought you would be out, Rupert,' he said. 'You were going to have such a busy day.'

'Well, yes, I know, Dan, but after what you said last night I felt we ought to learn a bit more about Peggy, so I've been talking to her.'

'That's good,' Dan said, 'but I wish you'd waited till we could talk together.' It was rare for Dan to rebuke him, and Rupert felt stung, but then Dan produced a letter from his pocket.

'This is for you,' he said, handing it over. Then he walked out of the room.

Rupert tore the letter open. He thought the handwriting was beautiful. It read:

Dear Rupert

I just wanted to thank you so much for that lovely, lovely picnic. I enjoyed it so much until I went and spoilt everything by my silly showing off. I want to thank you for your gentle care of me yesterday. You were so kind and considerate.

My ankle is less painful now and I am absolutely longing to get out in this lovely weather. My family are so busy, and I hope it isn't too much of a cheek to ask if you could spare some time one afternoon this week to push me in my wheelchair into the park, Bentham Park. It's lovely there, and it's not far from our house. I hope you can come.

    Yours gratefully
    Imogen.

Rupert ran upstairs to his room. He found he was shaking. He sat on his bed and read the letter again, and then again.
    How can I possibly refuse her? he thought.

CHAPTER ELEVEN

On the Thursday of the same week Dan found himself suffering from nostalgia. It only happened rarely because he was very happy in the big industrial town of Barnham, but just occasionally he felt an intense longing for the countryside, and in particular for the Ireland of his childhood.

It's probably the weather, he thought, the weather and the lovely time of year.

During the past week the days had been full of sunshine, and there was blossom everywhere, even in the small presbytery garden which Rupert tended. Dan remembered that on Monday, after visiting Imogen Moriarty, he had walked by Bentham Park and thought how inviting it looked. He decided to go out there that afternoon and try to recapture his joy in the beauty of nature.

The further he wandered into the park, the more beautiful he found it. There were a great many trees, and he found a little beech wood with a stream running through it. There were drifts of bluebells on the banks and the beech leaves were newly green. Birds were singing and sunlight was filtered through the branches. It was a peaceful place and there seemed to be nobody about except for a solitary young man sitting on a bench some distance away.

Dan sat on another bench and relaxed. He loved the solitude and the absence of intrusive sound. But then he began to wonder about the young man. There was something odd about him. On such a warm day he wore a black overcoat with the collar turned up and he sat with his head down.

'It's none of your business,' he told himself. 'Don't interfere'. Then thoughts of possible suicide entered his head. Weren't the statistics for young men appallingly high?

He sat for a few more minutes and then walked slowly towards the young man. The ground was soft and his feet made no sound so he was almost at the bench when the man caught sight of him. Immediately he stood and was about to run when Dan's voice made him pause. The priest spoke gently and made no attempt to move closer. There was no response to his 'Hello,' but he continued to smile and speak gently. 'May I sit with you please?' he said.

The young man still looked terrified but he moved along to make space for Dan. For a while the silence between them was tense, but then the young man spoke. 'The flowers are beautiful,' he said.

'Yes,' Dan agreed. 'It's my first time in this park. Do you come here often?' He spoke slowly because the young man's English was hesitant.

'I have been here some days,' he said, and then he looked Dan in the face for the first time. 'I have no place,' he said.

'No place? I don't understand.'

'I am a failed asylum seeker. I come from Zimbabwe. My father was killed and my mother was raped. But the Home Office will not believe me. I have no papers, no proof. When it happened I ran away. I was fifteen. Now they will deport me back to Zimbabwe. But I am afraid. I will be killed.'

Dan was stunned. He had read about such cases, and momentarily felt outraged as he often did at government policies, but this was different. This was a dreadful human dilemma touching his life, a young man living in terror sitting next to him.

For a moment he said nothing, and into his mind came the phrase 'Living Ghosts'. Of course, that's what this young man was. Someone who did not officially exist, who had no means of support, no access to benefit, no home and all the time the threat of deportation hanging over his head.

It was impossible to walk away. How could he pat this lad on the back and say 'Hope things work out for you,' and leave him there? If he did that he would be turning his back not only on the boy but on everything his ministry stood for: Christ-like compassion. He knew that if he took some action he would also be taking a considerable risk. Possibly he would be breaking the law and so bringing the priesthood into disrespect but he had hesitated long enough.

'Will you tell me your name?' he asked gently.

'Bede,' the boy said, then, panic showing suddenly in his eyes, 'but please don't …'

'No, no, don't worry, Bede,' Dan said, 'I want to help you.'

'Yes?' Bede sounded very doubtful.

'Yes,' said Dan firmly. 'First, tell me, do you have anywhere to sleep?'

'No, that's why I come here. It's a good place to hide.'

'And if it rains?'

Bede shrugged.

'When did you last eat anything?'

Bede shrugged again.

'Right, Bede. By the way, I like your name. But it sounds so English.' Dan was trying to get the boy to relax.

'Yes. They gave me this name at the Mission where I went to school. I was born on this saint's day, the 25th of May.'

'The English changed my name too,' Dan said, 'my name at home is Donal, but now it is Daniel. My friends call me Dan. I hope you will call me Dan, because I am taking you to my house, to stay there. It will be a safe place for you.'

Bede's eyebrows rose, but he said nothing.

'Stay here, please,' Dan said. 'I will go and bring my car to the park gates. Then I will come to fetch you. Okay?'

Bede still showed no emotion.

'Okay,' he said, and bent his head again, his hood hiding his face.

CHAPTER TWELVE

The same afternoon, in the same park, was, as far as Rupert was concerned, perfect. Here he was, alone with Imogen, in this beautiful place, the sun was shining, and she seemed as happy as he was.

She knew the park and was directing him as he wheeled her chair.

'I know a lovely spot, near the river,' she said. 'There'll be millions of bluebells this time of year. There are benches there too, so you can have a rest from pushing me around. It's so good of you, Rupert, and I feel so happy. Could you just stop for a moment?' She put her head back and looked up at him, a smile on her lips. 'It's a pity you're a priest,' she said.

Imogen stayed looking up at him, waiting for his response, and he looked down at her, overwhelmed by his feelings.

'Rupert!' the familiar voice was sharp and clear. Both young people started, both blushed.

'Dan!'

Dan stopped. He had been running and was panting a little. 'Hello, Imogen,' he said and without pausing, 'Look, Rupert, something's happened.'

Quickly he told them about his meeting with Bede and his promise to the boy.

'Will it be all right with you? To have him in the house, I mean? I'm sorry, I should have consulted you first. It's your home too ...'

Rupert felt shaken. Imogen was still in the forefront of his mind, and he didn't feel overly concerned about the issue of the refugee.

'Sure,' he said, yes, of course. I'll be glad to have Bede with us.'

'Good, I'm grateful, Rupert. It's not a little thing we're taking on. And Imogen, I know I can count on you not to say a word to anyone. That's very important.'

She looked grave and concerned. 'Of course, you can depend on me,' she said, 'oh, the poor, poor boy!'

Dan left them and began to jog towards the park gates.

For a day or two, Dan was preoccupied with Bede, trying to find a way of gently relaxing him from his traumatised state. Peggy did her part, cheerfully fussing over Bede, 'feeding him up' as she put it, surreptitiously bringing in clothes for him, some she bought herself and some given by Walter, who was used to his mother begging for things for some good cause or other. She shortened one or two of the garments Rupert had given him. They were of a similar build, but Rupert was considerably taller.

Dan had given Bede the room that had belonged to Mrs McNab, on the understanding that if any guests should arrive he would move up into the attic where Dan was.

After a few days, Dan began to feel more relaxed about Bede. So far he had shown little emotion, and only spoken when spoken to, but he held his head up and the tension in him seemed to have loosened a little. One night Dan found it was not worry over Bede that kept him awake, but anxiety over Rupert, Rupert and Imogen. Over and over again he tried to recall the moment he had surprised them in the park. He knew he had been wrought up himself, focused on the necessity of removing Bede to safety, so perhaps he had imagined the look that passed between the young couple just as he approached. 'Please, please,' he implored, in a desperate prayer, don't let Rupert be in love. Or Imogen for that matter.' But it wasn't the sort of prayer he really expected God to answer.

Dan knew the pain of being in love. He knew all about the dilemma of being a dedicated priest who was passionately in love with a woman. He wouldn't wish that on anyone, and especially not Rupert who was sensitive and vulnerable by nature and just beginning to emerge as a strong and effective priest. But suppose he was imagining all this? In any case, was it any of his business? Had he any right, or duty, to interfere in Rupert's life? He hardly slept, but Kate Moriarty's telephone call the next day was very welcome.

'Could I come round?' she asked. 'I think we need to talk about Imogen and Rupert.'

Dan was to some extent dismayed. So there was an 'Imogen and Rupert'. But he was also relieved that there was someone he could share his concern with.

Kate was forthright as usual.

'Imogen's far too young,' she said. 'She's eighteen, for goodness sake, with all her career ahead of her. She's already been accepted by two universities, if her grades are good enough. But will they be, if she's mooning around thinking only about wonderful Rupert?'

Dan surprised himself by coming to Rupert's defence. 'He's only twenty-five, Kate,' he said, 'Is seven years an unsurmountable difference?'

'You're surely not condoning this, are you Dan? I know you're an open, liberal sort of priest which frankly is why I like you, but I wouldn't have thought you would go as far as to encourage a priest to have an affair …?'

'Whoa, steady on, Kate,' Dan couldn't help laughing. 'You're getting carried away. Of course I don't want Rupert to break his vows and I'd hate to lose him as a priest, but I don't really see what I, or you for that matter, can do if they are really in love.'

'I'm afraid you're probably right,' Kate admitted. 'You know in a few years' time I'd be only too happy for Imogen and Rupert to marry. He's a very nice guy, there's no doubt. And it won't surprise you to know that I think it's absolutely ridiculous that priests have to be celibate. It's unnatural, and unfair, and it's certainly not ordained by God!'

Dan sighed, thinking, if only she knew how much he agreed with her. But he only said, 'Rupert's doing an awful lot of good here, you know. He would be a great loss to the parish.'

'And how on earth would he support her? What would they do for money?'

'I think we're getting a bit ahead of ourselves here, Kate. It's quite possible one or even both of them will grow out of these feelings. Imogen may decide her career is too important, or Rupert that the priesthood means too much to him. For me, the question is, do I say anything to Rupert?'

It was Kate's turn to sigh heavily.

'I guess not. And the same goes for me. We'll just have to sit it out and hope for the best, Dan. But it's a comfort for me that you agree with me. We both want the same outcome, don't we? A gradual fading away of this romance?'

Dan nodded. He was less certain. He thought, deep down, I just want Rupert to be happy and fulfilled.

CHAPTER THIRTEEN

As the months slipped by Bede gradually changed. He began to relate, first to Peggy, then to the others. He started to talk about his childhood and the place where he grew up. Sometimes he smiled or laughed. He spent his time reading and learning to play Walter's guitar which Peggy had given him. He helped around the house and read voraciously. Rupert brought him books twice a week from the library. He was scrupulously careful to disappear into his room whenever anyone called at the house.

But Bede was not perfectly happy. He often had a nightmares about his family and what had happened to them, and whenever he tried to imagine his future he found it impossible. He knew he couldn't stay in the presbytery for ever. The worst aspect of his day-to-day existence, however, was the feeling of imprisonment. Everyone in the house treated him kindly and thoughtfully, he was well-fed and comfortable, but he wasn't free. After a few months in the house he longed to go out and walk around, to feel the wind or the sun on his face and the grass, or even the pavement under his feet.

He confided all this to Rupert one evening, and from then on Rupert, and sometimes Imogen, too, would take him out after dark, to walk in one of the local parks.

In the meantime Wilfrid Drew had got over his disappointment at not being elected to the parish council. He felt ashamed of what he saw as his childish reaction on the night of the election. He was a man who found it hard to apologise, but slowly came to the conclusion, with Lydia's encouragement, that it would be good to make his peace with Father Dan. (Dan, as it happened, had forgotten all about the incident.)

Wilfrid had retired now, and had plenty of free time, so he chose to walk by the presbytery one afternoon on the off-chance of finding the priest in. He rang the doorbell and knocked on the door two or three times and then, receiving no answer, on a sudden impulse he went round to the sitting room window and peered in. To his astonishment, he saw a black youth sitting on the sofa absorbed in a book. Wilfrid tapped on the window, but the boy dropped the book and ran from the room. Wilfrid waited for him to open the door but nothing happened.

Mystified, and forgetting about his intended apology, Wilfrid determined to tackle Dan about this at the next opportunity. That evening he telephoned the presbytery and made an appointment to see him. Bede had not appeared for supper and wasn't there for breakfast either. Peggy went upstairs and tapped on his door. When he opened it, she saw his look of fear.

'What is it?' she asked.

'Yesterday a man came. He looked in the window and saw me. I'm afraid to come out now.'

Peggy decided not to put pressure on him. 'Don't worry, Bede. I'm sure it will be all right. I'll bring you a cooked breakfast to make up for no supper last night.' And so she did.

When Wilfrid questioned him, Dan felt he had no alternative but to tell him the truth. Wilfrid looked gravely concerned.

'Look, Father,' he said, 'I realise you have acted out of compassion. But don't you think you should consider the consequences?'

'What consequences?'

'Well, I think you might be breaking the law. Certainly you would if the immigration people came and you wouldn't let them in. And so, if you're found out, you could be in all sorts of trouble. There could be a big scandal, and none of us wants that, do we?'

'Wilfrid, can't you put yourself in the shoes of this poor young lad?'

'Well, I know it's hard for him, but ….'

'I'm sorry,' Dan was trying to curb his anger. 'I can't listen to this …'

Wilfrid shrugged and left.

Lydia was sympathetic.

'Poor darling,' she said to Wilfrid, 'he really should have listened to you. You are a lawyer after all and you're only trying to help him. It would be awful if he lost his job. You know, I much preferred Canon Murphy, but Father Dan has done a lot of good and people seem really happy with him.'

'Well, I don't see what we can do,' Wilfrid was gloomy. 'If you ask me, he's his own worst enemy.'

Lydia was quiet for a moment, thinking.

'There is one thing you can do,' she said.

'What's that?'

'Well, you'll be seeing the bishop on Thursday, won't you, at your Old Boys reunion? What about a word in his ear?'

Wilfrid was shocked.

'I can't do that, Lydia' he said. 'Father Dan trusts me.'

'Did you promise not to tell anyone?'

'No, but …'

'Well, then. At least think about it, Will.'

The bishop had known Wilfrid for a long time. He respected him but found him a little too officious and was not pleased when Wilfrid took him into a corner and told him that Father Dan was harbouring a refugee whom the Home Office wanted to deport. He thanked Wilfrid rather curtly.

Later that day he brooded on this news. He did like

Dan Spring and knew he was doing some very good work, but he saw him as something of a threat to the smooth running of the diocese. You could never be sure if or when Dan would step out of line and now he had gone and done it.

According to Wilfrid, Dan wasn't exactly breaking the law, but if the immigration officers came seeking this boy and Dan resisted them, then he could really be in trouble, and wouldn't that put the diocese in a bad light? Wouldn't it be a cause of scandal? Of course Dan was well known for letting his heart rule his head, but that wasn't always a bad thing. This poor lad from Zimbabwe, the bishop thought, I must pray for him tonight.

Next morning he telephoned Dan and told him that whereas he sympathised with the boy's predicament, he felt bound, as his bishop, to advise Dan to let him go.

'I'll think about it,' was all Dan said, and think about it was what he did, for several hours. He was in no doubt that it was Wilfrid who had told the bishop about Bede, but he didn't want to waste time indulging in his anger. He had to weigh up what to do. It was his duty to obey the bishop, but the bishop hadn't given him an order, only advice. Even so, to keep Bede would be an act of defiance. But he had to be honest, what would he do if immigration officials arrived on his doorstep? He could hardly fend them off physically. Now that their secret had leaked to Wilfrid and presumably Lydia, how long would it be before the immigration people found out? And if it came to confrontation, wouldn't that be more harrowing for Bede than a gentle explanation from him as to why he had to leave? Or would that be worse?

He was weary of his tormented thoughts and decided to seek some relief by sharing his worries with Rupert, always a willing listener. But the willing listener was out, presumably listening to Imogen, Dan thought wryly. Not sure whether Peggy had gone home, he went into the kitchen where he found her putting on her coat.

'Could you spare a minute, Peg?' he asked.

She saw the troubled look on his face.

'Sure,' she said, 'what's up, Dan?'

He told her and she listened without interrupting. Then she said, 'That's too bad. The bishop's really put you on the spot, hasn't he?'

'Oh, Peg, I just can't tell Bede to go,' he said. 'I don't care what the bishop says or does, I could never bring myself to do that.' 'No,' Peg said, 'I don't think you could.'

Dan smiled at her. 'Thanks for listening.' And then he went back to his room. Peggy said a quick prayer and took a deep breath. Then she went up to Bede's room and tapped on his door. He let her in and she talked to him for a long time.

Then she went home.

The next morning Bede didn't come down to breakfast. Rupert went to call him and found his room empty. The bed was neatly made, his guitar and all his clothes gone.

'He's gone! Bede – he's gone, he's left!'

He saw the shock on Dan's face, tears running down Peggy's cheeks. After a moment Dan went over to Peggy and put his arms round her.

'Peg? You did this, didn't you? You did it because I couldn't!'

Peggy nodded. She dried her eyes. 'Yes, I thought it best. It's all right, though, Dan, Rupert. He seemed to understand. I gave him a holdall and quite a lot of food. He was very dignified. Poor lamb ...' She began to cry then.

It was a time of mourning for them all. For over a week Dan ate little and slept little. It seemed to him that everything was his fault.

It was several weeks before the letter came. It was addressed to:

Father Dan
Presbitry
Barnham
England.

And inside was a letter:

Dear Sir,
I am the uncle of Bede. He was living with me and
my family safe. But a car nocked him down and kill
him. Before he die he wrote this leter so I am sending
to you.
Yours faithfully,
Joseph Mtetwi

Another letter was enclosed:

Dear Dan, Rupert and Peggy,
I write to say thank you. You all gave me a good and
happy time and I will remember you as long as I
live. Peggy was like my mother.
Yours faithfully,
Bede.

They all wept, as did Imogen when Rupert showed her the
letters.

CHAPTER FOURTEEN

In the meantime the parish was thriving. There was a lot more lay activity and all the different groups increased their membership. Every Sunday the work produced by the children in their own group was taken up in the offertory procession and displayed for everyone to admire. The choir learnt several new hymns and the folk group sang at one of the Masses every Sunday. Ben Shaw and Ernest Gage started a parish walk which took place each Sunday after Mass. People with cars drove others out to the starting place and the walk proved an excellent source for mingling people from different ages and backgrounds.

Oliver Hardy, once renowned as a pessimist, was galvanised with enthusiasm when Dan asked him to organise special celebrations for people from different cultures, and Norah McGinty took on the job of his assistant. These evenings were spread through the year: there was a Caribbean party, a Chinese party, an Irish party, a Scottish and a Polish one. People cooked or brought their native food, wore their national costumes, sang their national songs and danced their national dances. It was all real 'craic' as Norah said, and everyone was welcome at these events.

In addition to all this, the Justice & Peace Group, newly formed with Kate Moriarty as its Chair, organised events for Peace Sunday, Homeless Sunday, Racial Justice Sunday and Human Rights Day. And at Christmas, Sister Lucy, one of the teachers at the parish school, wrote a Nativity play for the children.

Musing on all this, Dan said to Rupert, 'You know, if it weren't for the sacraments, I could easily retire!'

'Yes,' Rupert agreed, 'though I think people still like us to visit.'

Lydia Drew had a conscience. She was impulsive and often took action without carefully thinking it through. One day Dan showed her the letter from Zimbabwe and that set her thinking, 'I was too hasty. I should never have pushed Wilfrid into sneaking on Father Dan to the Bishop. I wish I had given it all more thought, been more compassionate towards that young man.'

It was while thinking about this that Lydia got her inspiration. There's something I could do, she thought. I could give a party, a big party for refugees and people seeking asylum. We could take over The Manor and get people to bring food. The Manor was a local hotel that was often hired for parties. I'm sure loads of people would help. And we could buy presents for the children …

She couldn't wait to tell Wilfrid of her plans, but it took him a while to be enthused. 'I suppose we could get a live band, use the Youth Club,' he said. 'Father Rupert tells me they're pretty good, especially that ferocious-looking fellow, Basher, I think they call him.'

'Well, yes,' Lydia agreed, 'but couldn't we also invite the guests to entertain us? They could sing or play their instruments or do whatever they do,' she ended vaguely.

'Darling, do you really think we could manage all this?'

'Yes, yes, of course. We'll have loads of help. It just needs someone with good organisational skills.'

Wilfrid grinned. 'And that means you! Do you know, Lydia, I'm beginning to look forward to it!'

The party was held on the 29th of June. Lydia didn't tell more than a dozen people that it happened to be her birthday. 'The feast of St Peter and St Paul. If I'd been born a boy I would have been Peter Paul, as it is I'm Lydia Petra Paula.' Norah McGinty, overhearing this as she worked alone in the kitchen, sorting out the food people had brought, muttered softly, 'It happens to be my birthday too.' So it was a great surprise when after they had all sung for Lydia, the band struck up again, singing 'Happy Birthday, dear Norah' and then Cody Shuttleworth came over to her with a beautifully wrapped parcel. Lydia had been given flowers, and now she made a gracious speech of thanks. Norah said nothing, just smiled, and took her parcel home to unwrap. It was a little brooch in the shape of a dove. Normally Norah didn't wear jewellery, but she was delighted with her unexpected present and immediately pinned it on her coat.

But this was only an interlude in an evening of great celebration. First the Youth Club Band performed to great acclaim. Basher's drumming was appreciated by most people but that night the star of the band was a pale, thin lad called Tony Paley, who played the guitar almost like a professional.

However, the evening belonged to the asylum seekers, who provided various kinds of entertainment, depending on their country of origin. It was a beautiful midsummer night and people wandered out into the garden. Lydia kept calm even when a china cup that had belonged to her mother was broken. Observing this incident, Dan, who had just arrived with Rupert, said, 'Lydia, you are magnificent!' He nodded and managed a smile across to Wilfrid, but he was still hurt and angry at what he saw as the man's betrayal and its tragic result.

CHAPTER FIFTEEN

Some months after the news of Bede's death, Imogen decided it was the time to have a serious talk with her parents. She waited till the smaller children were in bed and her older siblings occupied with their various interests, then told her parents she needed to talk to them both.

They could see that Imogen was tense and anxious, so Robbie said 'Let's go into the sitting room where we won't be disturbed. I'll make a pot of tea.'

As soon as they were all seated, Imogen began, 'I'm going to marry Rupert.'

There was a moment's silence, then Robbie said 'Darling, are you sure? Aren't you a bit young? Have you really thought it through?'

'Oh, Dad, I've hardly thought of anything else for over a year. And I'm absolutely positive. It's what I want, it's what I need, and it's what Rupert needs.'

'Well,' said Kate, 'I can't pretend to be surprised, Imogen, and I won't pretend to be pleased. I was so hoping you would come to see how rash this is, how you're throwing your life away ...'

'Hey, steady on Kate,' Robbie interrupted. 'I think that's a bit strong. How is she throwing her life away?'

'She's only nineteen, and she's highly intelligent. She could go far in almost any career she chose. She hardly knows anything. Think of the experiences she could have, the people she could meet ...'

'I won't meet anyone as wonderful as Rupert, Mum. And by marrying him, I won't be cutting myself off from experiences. There are all sorts of interesting things we can do together. In fact, as soon as we're married, we're going to travel round the world together. Rupert's uncle has left him a generous amount of money and we intend to work in African and South American countries where we can be useful.'

Kate was surprised and impressed, but not entirely convinced.

'Imogen,' she said, 'when it comes down to it, all I want for you is fulfilment and happiness. I know your love for Rupert is not schoolgirl infatuation and I know that for someone of your age you have a wise head on your shoulders, but …'

For once Kate was inarticulate.

Robbie smiled at her.

'Could it be that like me, you don't want to lose your precious daughter? Are we being a bit selfish here?'

'Oh, no!' Imogen was dismayed. 'Don't say that! Nobody could be less selfish than you two. I'm just so sorry that this is upsetting for you both.'

'No, Immo, Robbie is right,' Kate said firmly. 'I certainly don't want to lose you, but I also want you to be happy. We know Rupert, and like him a lot, and I guess he's the one for you.'

'Oh, Mum,' Imogen was crying and laughing at the same time. 'Thank you, it means so much to me.' She hugged them both, then ran from the room and up to her bedroom, where she picked up the phone to dial Rupert.

Rupert was also in his bedroom, pacing up and down, trying to screw up the courage to face Dan. When Imogen told him her news, he was delighted for her, but he couldn't help thinking that his interview with Dan was going to be much more fraught and difficult than hers with her parents.

'I'm so glad,' he said.

'You sound very tense, though.'

'Yes, I'm just about to break the news to Dan.'

'Oh Rupert, don't worry. He's such a lovely man, I'm sure it will be all right.'

'I don't know, Imogen, I wish I had your confidence.'

Rupert had made an appointment to see Dan at nine o'clock in his office. Since there had never been such a formal arrangement between them before, Dan had a pretty good idea of what this was about. He had prayed and thought so hard about Rupert and Imogen for several months, but he still had no idea what his response would be.

Punctually at nine o'clock Rupert tapped on the office door and entered. He was clearly nervous and apprehensive, so Dan made an effort to put him at his ease.

'Sit down, Rupert,' he said. 'Whatever you've come to tell me, I'm not going to eat you.'

'Thanks. I know. It's just …' he paused and swallowed. 'I need to tell you, Imogen and I have decided to get married.'

He forced himself to look at Dan's face.

Dan neither smiled or frowned, but he did sigh.

'Oh dear,' he said, 'I have to say I'm sorry, Rupert. I'm sorry because I believed you had a true vocation, because you're already a very good priest, but most of all, to be honest, because I shall miss you so much.' He paused. 'I won't ask if you've thought this through; I know you better than that.'

'Oh Dan, I've agonised over it for so long. Believe me, at first I fought against it as hard as I could. But when I realised that Imogen felt the same way, I couldn't fight any more. How could I break her heart when I loved her so much? I know I can't expect you to understand, Dan. You don't know what it is to be in love …'

'What makes you think that?' Dan said, quite sharply.

Rupert felt his face redden. 'I'm sorry, I didn't think, I didn't know …' he stammered.

'It's all right, Rupert. How could you possibly know? I

shouldn't have jumped on you like that. But as you might guess, it's rather a sensitive issue.' He paused for a moment. ' It's quite a long time ago now, but it's very clear in my memory. I did fall in love, with a wonderful woman, and I know she loved me too.' He paused again.

'But your priesthood came first?' Rupert asked.

Dan smiled. 'I can't honestly say,' he said. 'But her marriage came first. And of course that's as it should be. I assure you, Rupert, I do know what it's like to be deeply in love, the heaven and the hell of it.'

'Believe me, Dan, I've prayed and prayed about this. I feel ashamed to think of my vows, and all the people I'll be letting down.'

'I understand,' said Dan, 'but now you've made up your mind, I suggest you continue to do your best as a priest, and at the same time, make plans for your future. It would be a pity if there was any shadow of guilt or shame on your wedding day. Perhaps you and Imogen have already made some decisions about that?'

'Well, yes, we have,' Rupert admitted. 'We're going to be married by my father in the church at Appledown, next Easter Monday, and we very much hope you will be there and give us your blessing.'

Dan smiled warmly. 'I would love to, Rupert,' he said. He rose to his feet and Rupert did the same, extending his hand to shake Dan's. But Dan folded him in an embrace.

'I'll certainly miss you,' he said, 'but I wish you all the happiness in the world.'

CHAPTER SIXTEEN

Dan had mixed feelings about hearing confessions. In the old days as a young priest he found he learned a great deal in his role as confessor, in particular he learned greater humility and admiration for the sinners who came to him. But nowadays very few people came and it seemed always to be the same people, two or three of the sisters from the convent, an old man and three old women who were regulars and seemed to Dan to lead blameless lives, certainly compared with his own.

This Saturday instead of taking his breviary or a book of spiritual reading, he took along a detective story. He felt slightly guilty about this, but excused himself on the grounds that, a) he had reached an especially crucial point of the story and b) if he didn't read something stimulating he would fall asleep as he had been called out the night before to the deathbed of a parishioner.

The regulars were punctual and so he had a good half hour to enjoy his novel.

He was almost on the last page when he had to put the book down hastily because someone had entered the confessional. Dan waited. Nothing happened, but then he became aware that the person on the other side of the grill was weeping. Once or twice she began to speak but each time her sobbing overcame her.

'I'm sorry, Father … Father, I can't …'

After two or three such falterings, Dan decided the poor woman had had enough of this. He spoke gently. 'My dear, please come out of the box. Confession is over now, but let me take you over to the house. It might be easier for you there and with a cup of tea inside you.'

It wasn't so much the words he said as the kindness in his voice that moved the woman to a fresh outbreak of sobbing, but she stumbled out of the confessional and followed Dan to the presbytery. She declined the offer of a drink, but sank into a chair near the fire.

Dan waited. The woman blew her nose and dried her eyes and began:

'You don't know me, Father, but I came to you because people tell me you're a kind man and not afraid to break the rules sometimes.'

'I don't know about that,' Dan began, but as though he had not spoken, the woman continued, 'My name is Deirdre Mulligan. I live on the Meadowfields Estate, and we are Catholics but don't get to Mass much. The trouble is, Father, I'm pregnant and I already have four children under six and the youngest, Rosie, has Downs Syndrome. She needs a lot of looking after.' Deirdre paused. She swallowed and sat up straight, determined not to cry.

'Father, I can't have this baby. I absolutely can't. I know I couldn't manage. I can't manage as it is. Please, please tell me it's all right in this case for me to have an abortion?'

Dan said nothing. He felt out of his depth. Silently, he prayed a desperate prayer. Then he said, 'What does your husband think, Deirdre?'

'He says I'm to get rid of it,' she said. 'He says I'm a fool if I don't and I can expect no help from him if I don't.'

Dan tried to hide the shock he felt. 'I can see this makes it very difficult for you,' he said.

'It doesn't make any difference what Derek says. He never gives me any help anyway. But the truth is, Father, I can't afford another child.'

Dan felt nervous now, knowing next to nothing about poverty. He said, 'Doesn't the Family Allowance or whatever it's called, help?'

Deirdre sounded better now. 'No, because Derek takes all the money he can lay his hands on and spends it on drink. It's as much as I can do to hide away a few pounds a week before he gets hold of it. We're desperate, Father, and I don't know what to do. Please, isn't the church meant to care about people? Couldn't you just say that in my case it would be all right to have an abortion?'

Dan longed to say yes to this poor woman, but how could he? If he did as she wanted, he would be betraying his priesthood, losing his integrity.

After a moment he spoke. 'I'm sorry, Deirdre, but I can't do as you ask. It's not up to me, it's up to you. You must do what you think is right. But have you thought about adoption?'

'It's no good thinking about that, Father. Derek would go mad if I even mentioned that idea. You may think that doesn't make much sense, but you don't know Derek.' She stood up and with great dignity said, 'Thank you, Father,' and then she left.

Afterwards, Dan wondered if there had been irony in that remark.

CHAPTER SEVENTEEN

The following day Dan was alone in the house. Peggy had long gone home and Rupert, as was his custom on Sundays, was out somewhere with Imogen. Dan enjoyed his Sunday evenings; they were usually the most peaceful of the week. So he was somewhat startled when someone not only rang the doorbell but banged on the door very loudly.

He opened it to find a large, angry man on his doorstep. He was also very obviously drunk. Before the priest could say anything he shouted: 'You murderer! You've killed her, that's what! You and your holy rules. You that think you understand anything about family life when you know damn all! Well, you've done it now. You've murdered my Deirdre, and how am I to manage now? She told me, see, what you said to her. You said it was up to her, didn't you? Well, that's what she did. She bloody well hanged herself this afternoon when the kids was at their Nan's. And who was it had to find her? Me, Muggins, of course. Didn't give a thought to how it would be for me, did she? And it's all your fault, Mr Holy Roman Poofter, so you can take this!'

Dan had listened to this tirade with growing horror, but now, as he saw the man lift a baseball bat and move closer, he just froze. He couldn't move so the bat hit him with full force on his head. He collapsed to the floor and his assailant slammed the door shut and fled.

Rupert was late home that night. As he tried to open the door he was surprised to find the light on and then something obstructing the door. When he managed to squeeze his head round the door he saw Dan lying in a pool of blood. Rupert was nearly sick. He more or less pulled himself together and rushed round to the back door for which he had the key and into the hall. He used his mobile phone to dial 999 and asked for an ambulance and the police, then he knelt and felt Dan's pulse. To his enormous relief he could feel its beating. But what should he do next? So far he had managed to keep calm but he could sense panic taking over. He needed to tell someone else, someone more experienced, more sensible. He dialled Peggy's number.

It was after midnight and she was fast asleep but she managed to get to the presbytery inside fifteen minutes. She found the paramedics talking to Rupert who looked ashen and distraught. She was deeply shocked to see the state Dan was in, unconscious and with so much blood round his body.

'How bad is he?' she asked the paramedics. 'Bad enough,' one replied. The other spoke more kindly, 'We'll know better when we get him to hospital. Would one of you like to come in the ambulance?'

Peggy looked at Rupert. He was white and tears were flowing. He was visibly shaking and his trouser bottoms were soaked in blood. 'I'll come,' she said. 'Rupert, you're not fit to drive, my dear. If you want to come to the hospital take a taxi. Or better, give the Moriartys a ring. I'm sure Robbie will be happy to take you. And while you're waiting, put on some clean trousers and make yourself a nice cup of tea with plenty of sugar.' So saying, Peggy left in the ambulance.

Rupert felt he was a wimp, acting like a pathetic small boy, but he followed Peggy's instructions and was relatively calm when Robbie arrived. Meanwhile the police had questioned him and examined the scene very thoroughly. One of them, carefully slipping the bloodstained baseball bat lying near the door into a plastic bag said, 'I don't think this is going to be too hard to crack.' Nor was it. The police already held Derek Mulligan's DNA on file since the first of his drunken brawls, so he was brought in for questioning the following day.

CHAPTER EIGHTEEN

It was also the following day, a Monday, that Dan came round from his temporary coma. He woke to find himself lying in a hospital bed and was astonished. The next thing he knew, a smiling nurse was looking down at him.

'Hello, Father,' she said, 'welcome back to the world!' He smiled back, recognising one of his parishioners, 'Maggie!' he said. ' But what happened? Why am I here? I don't remember …' but even as he said it, he did begin to remember. His face fell and his speech was agitated. 'Oh dear, yes. It's terrible. Oh, poor Deirdre …'

Maggie Whelan tried to calm him. 'It's all right, Father, there's nothing to worry about.'

'Oh but there is, Maggie. It's the worst that could have happened and it's all my fault. I must go …' He tried to get out of bed, but the nurse restrained him, at the same time calling for help. He was mildly sedated and later that day, when he was awake, a doctor came and sat by his bed.

'You've had a very lucky escape, Father' he said. 'That was a really nasty blow to your head and it will take a while to heal, but no serious, lasting damage has been done, and thankfully, your brain function has not been affected. However, it's going to hurt for a week or so and we'll keep you on something to lessen the pain but you'll have to stay here for at least seven days while we keep an eye on you. When you go home you will have to promise us that you will rest and not take on any sort of work for a month.'

Dan took all this with lowering spirits, but he was too sleepy to react strongly. For a few days he was only allowed one visitor at a time and that was usually Rupert. The bishop was away in Rome and sent a message of condolence. So many people phoned the hospital to ask about Dan that the lines became blocked, so Peggy undertook to field all such calls and she agreed to sleep at the presbytery until Dan was well enough to come home.

But unfortunately, Dan seemed to be making very little progress. His wound was healing nicely, but he seemed sunk in an impregnable gloom. Rupert, and Peggy, on the few occasions she visited him in hospital, tried every way they could think of to get him to sit up, read, eat some of the chocolates and grapes people had sent him, listen to the radio, all to no avail. Dan mostly lay flat on his bed with his eyes closed and when he spoke it was always to blame himself for what had happened to Deirdre.

Dan was not himself. He had lost his bearings; he could no longer pray. It was as though the scaffolding which had supported him through every crisis had collapsed.

All his life he had relied on the discipline of personal prayer. He was only too aware that he was not a naturally organised person, and had therefore made sure that, come what may, he set aside at least fifteen minutes twice every day to be still and quiet before God. This was in addition to the official morning and evening prayer of the church. When he first got up, and just before he went to bed, he kept what he thought of as space to be with God.

His prayer was silent, attentive, but he also quite often asked for something: the courage to face whatever might happen in the day or sensitivity towards people he might meet. And his prayer at night was full of thankfulness and intercession for people whose lives he had touched during that day. Even so, he tried to spend most of this treasured time simply being open to God.

But now, in hospital, as soon as he realised what had happened to Deirdre, he was so deeply immersed in guilt and shame that he found it impossible to pray, to connect with the God he had trusted and loved for so long. Rupert and Peggy could not understand what had happened to him. They were both equally distressed and concerned.

'There must be something we can do' Peggy said. 'This is so completely unlike him, absolutely out of character.' They sat for a moment in silence, each of them brooding on the situation, each of them desperate to find a way of restoring Dan to his usual positive self. Then Rupert said, 'I've thought of something, Peggy, that just might help. We know Dan has no near family left alive except his old mother in Ireland, but once or twice he's mentioned a particular priest friend, I think he's a monk, a Benedictine or a Dominican, and he's called Anselm. I know Dan thinks highly of him and likes him a lot. Would it be worth trying to get hold of him and seeing if he would come over?'

Peggy was smiling for the first time in days. 'That's a brilliant idea, Rupert,' she said. 'Why didn't I think of it? Anselm would be the man to lift Dan's spirits if anyone can. I've met him a couple of times when he came over to see Dan. He'll be in the Diocesan Directory. Go on, Rupert, get in touch with him now!'

This Rupert did and Dom Anselm arrived two days later at the presbytery where Rupert filled him in with what had happened as far as he could. Rupert took Anselm to the hospital and left him with Dan. Dan briefly opened his eyes and gave a weary half smile. 'Oh, it's you, Anselm,' he said. 'There's nothing wrong with me. You shouldn't have come all this way, but thanks.' Then he closed his eyes and turned his head away.

'Come on, Dan, sit up, and let me look at you properly!' Anselm said, and it was an order rather than a plea.

Reluctantly, Dan did sit up, and uncomfortably met his friend's gaze. Anselm said nothing, and after a while Dan spoke. 'Look, Anselm, the life has gone out of me. They must have told you what I did. I just can't get the image of that poor Deirdre hanging herself out of my head. I don't want to sit up and get better.' He looked as though he was about to cry. ' Anselm, the guilt is terrible!'

Anselm spoke more gently now. 'Look Dan, ' he said, 'I think I understand. But just look at yourself, mate. You're wallowing in guilt like some people wallow in self-pity. In your case it's a complete waste of time.'

Dan had begun to come to life. 'But she was such a poor suffering young woman, Anselm. I could have so easily said it was all right, in her situation, to have a termination, couldn't I?'

'No, you know you couldn't, certainly not easily. The way things stand, no priest could have said that, however grim the circumstances; certainly I couldn't.'

Dan was more like himself now. 'But wouldn't you, wouldn't you have felt terrible if the young woman killed herself? Wouldn't you feel responsible for her death?'

'I don't know. I just can't say how I would feel, except I know I would feel bloody angry with the man who had ruined my handsome face, even if only temporarily. You've got an impressive scar there, Dan.'

Dan actually laughed, and Anselm took heart.

'I understand the couple had four small children, one of them disabled,' he said. 'Their mother is dead, and their father's probably going to prison. Have you been too guilty to think about them?'

But Dan was already flinging off the bedding and getting to his feet.

'Oh,no! What a fool, what a self-centred bastard I've been! Anselm, help me, please. Could you phone Peg at the presbytery and get her to bring me my clothes ... but tell me, do you know where those poor children are?'

'Steady on, Dan, they're perfectly all right. Peggy told me they're with a family called Moriarty. I expect you know them?'

Dan's relief was evident. 'Oh, thank God, that's good.' He paused, and Anselm couldn't interpret the look on his face. 'Oh, Anselm,' he said, 'I said, "thank God", didn't I? And I really meant it. Now I can pray again!' In answer, Anselm smiled and raised his eyebrows. Then he sang, softly, the first line of a hymn they both knew well: 'O Love, that will not let me go.'

'You surely hadn't forgotten that, had you, Dan?'

Dan grinned. 'Just temporary insanity,' he said, 'I feel … but never mind how I feel, we've got to lose no time in finding those children a proper home. Kate Moriarty is some kind of saint, but she's for ever involved in good works. I know she's worn out as it is. We must find them a really good foster home where they can all be together. But if they can be happy anywhere, they'll be happy with Kate. The thing is, Anselm, I must get home and start finding somewhere for them.'

Anselm was more or less listening to this as he was dialling the presbytery number.

He drove Dan home and stayed with him in the presbytery for two nights. 'I can see you two are ecstatic to have the old rogue back to normal,' he said to Peggy and Rupert, 'but please do your best to make him take time over changing the world! He needs rest.'

Rupert and Peggy promised to do their best.

CHAPTER NINETEEN

The day Anselm left, Dan went round to see the Moriartys. Deliberately, he hadn't warned Kate that he was coming, and it was just as he had expected.

He arrived at teatime, and he found the whole family, except for Robbie, who was at work and Kate and Imogen who were standing, seated round the kitchen table. Imogen was buttering tea-cakes and Kate was helping Rosie, the smallest Mulligan child, to feed. The house was even more chaotic than usual: there was a pile of dishes waiting to be washed, and two large plastic bags of dirty clothes waiting to be dealt with in one corner. Barney, now a toddler, sat smiling in his high chair, jam all over his face.

Kate gave him her usual warm welcome. 'I'm sorry, Dan, all the chairs in here are in use, but if you go through to the sitting room, where at least for the moment it's quiet, I'll bring you a cup of tea and some tea-cakes.'

Dan did as she suggested and soon afterwards Kate came in with the tea and sat down opposite him.

'It's good to see you looking so well, Dan,' she said, then, smiling she added, 'That's a really impressive scar you have there!'

Dan laughed. 'So everyone says. I keep brushing my hair down over it in the hope of keeping it hidden, but it just doesn't work. But how are you, Kate? You don't look well at all. And surely you've lost weight?'

'Oh, I'm fine, Dan. I just get a bit tired, that's all. The Mulligan kids are as good as gold, too good if you ask me, but all four of the poor little things wet the bed every night, and Johnny, the eldest, is developing a stammer.'

Dan was concerned. 'How long are you thinking of keeping the Mulligans here?' 'Oh, I don't know, I haven't even thought about that. They can stay indefinitely. They're well …, they're as happy as can be expected, I suppose. They know me, you see. I used to go round to see Deirdre quite often. In fact I suggested she should come to see you when she was so worried about her pregnancy. But obviously she didn't.'

For a few seconds, Dan felt the resurgence of his overwhelming guilt, but silently he told himself: This is not about you, it's about the children and Kate.

'Kate,' he said, 'it's wonderful what you're doing. Obviously what Johnny and the others need more than anything is love, and you give it to them in spades. But – and I'm sorry to say this – I think it's too much for you.' He saw that he was making her angry, but he went on, 'Let me ask you a few questions.' She nodded reluctantly.

'Right. Do you still visit the hospital regularly?' 'Yes.'

'Do you still visit the prison regularly?' 'Yes.'

'Are you a member of the Justice and Peace Group?' 'Yes.'

'Do you clean the church?' 'No! I've given that up, I'm afraid.'

'Good. Are you a Samaritan?' 'Yes. How did you know that?'

'Never mind. Do you write for the local newspaper?' 'Yes.'

'Do you have a husband and children of your own who need your care and attention?' 'Yes. You know I do. And I know I do, honestly, Dan.'

'Well, Kate, now we've come to it, the last question and the crunch question: Are you aware of you own limitations?'

Kate stared at him. Then she said, 'I don't know whether to laugh or cry.'

'Well, I've just learned a hard lesson about myself,' Dan

said, ' so we could try laughing.' And they did, until Kate said, 'I know you're right, Dan. I do take on far too much. But, you know, it would break my heart if those children were to go into Care. And I couldn't bear it if they were split up. But I suppose you think we should contact Social Services?'

'Yes, I do,' Dan said, 'and if you don't mind I'd like to be involved. But before I go, could we go back into the kitchen? I'd like to get to know Deirdre's children.'

Afterwards, as Kate was letting him out of the house, she said, 'I guess they miss their father too, you know, brute though he is. I simply can't imagine why he attacked you, though, Dan. Perhaps he has a grudge against the church?'

Dan smiled. 'You could say that. I'm not pressing charges so he can see his children, but we do need to find someone else to look after them.'

CHAPTER TWENTY

The people at Social Services were not encouraging. The pleasant woman Kate and Dan went to see shook her head. 'Those poor kids!' she said, 'I saw their pictures in the paper, but we have nobody on our books who would be willing to take them, not all four of them. We did have a lady who would have been just right for them, Glory Tattershall. We were all so sad when she told us she was retiring from fostering last year. But I'm in contact with other areas, and I'll let you know as soon as anything comes up.'

As the days went by Dan worried about Kate and felt increasingly frustrated to have no news from Social Services although he knew he was being unrealistic, as the numbers of people prepared to foster families was so limited. Then about a fortnight later he answered the door and opened it to find himself staring at what he later told Peggy was a vision.

The vision was female and black. She had a huge frame and towered over Dan. She also had a huge smile of gleaming white teeth. On her head was a turban of gold, purple and orange silk,and the rest of her was covered by a vast garment made of yellow silk reaching to her toes.

'Hello, Father Daniel Spring,' she said, and her voice was musical. 'My name is Glory Tattershall. May I come in?'

'Oh yes, of course. Please do come in, Glory. And please call me Dan.'

She entered the house and walked gracefully after him. He called Peggy to ask her to bring coffee and biscuits, and when they were both seated he asked Glory, 'What can I do for you?' She gave a deep, rich chuckle. 'I am not a Roman Catholic,' she said, ' I go to the Pentecostal Church. But my friend told me you are looking for a foster mother for those little kids that lost their mother so tragically.'

'Well,yes, I am hoping we can find someone. But I'm not in any way an official in this. I'm just trying to help. If you are interested, you should contact Social Services.'

Glory chuckled again. 'Oh, that's funny,' she said, 'Social Services contacted me.'

'Oh!' was all Dan could manage in response.

'Yes, you see I have been a foster mother in Barnham for thirty years, but last year I was sixty and everybody said I should retire. So I did. But I don't like it. So when I heard about this family I was wishing I could help, and then I was so happy when Social Services contacted me. They told me about you, and I knew about you because I have many friends who come to your church and they like you and they say you are a good man.' Seeing Dan's embarrassment, she laughed. ' So I thought it would be a kindness to show you my letters and photographs of my boys and girls, to give you some idea about me. Then you will perhaps be able to decide if I would be suitable for this family, to make them happy.'

'It's not for me to decide, Glory,' Dan said, 'but I'm grateful to you for putting me in the picture, and I feel a whole lot better for meeting you.'

As this point Peggy came in with the coffee and biscuits. With surprising grace, Glory got to her feet and enfolded Peggy in an embrace. 'Peggy! It's so good to see you, man. You work here? That's good.'

Peggy grinned. 'It's really good to see you, too, Glory. It's been a long time. I'd heard you had retired?'

'Well, I had, Peg, but now I'm thinking …'

'Oh yes!' Peggy cried, 'the little Mulligans. You'd take them? You know one of them has Downs?'

'Yes, I know that. I have a soft spot for children with Downs Syndrome.' She turned to Dan. 'But I have taken up too much of your time, Dan. I have brought you my collection.' She put her hand into her capacious bag and drew out a thick file which she handed to him. 'Please study it, carefully,' she added, 'and take good care of it and don't lend it to anyone.' She paused. 'Or you could let that Mrs Moriarty see it, if you think it would make her feel better. I heard she's doing a good job with the children and from what I hear she will not want to give them up. Thanks for the coffee. I'm sorry I didn't drink it, but I guess we are both busy people!'

When the door closed behind Glory, Dan sat down. He drank two cups of coffee, then looked up to see Peggy watching and grinning.

'What do you think?' she asked.

'I think she's wonderful,' Dan said.

'Do you reckon I could have a peek at some of those things in that file?'

'I reckon you could, Peggy.'

Glory's file was fascinating. Most of the letters were from children who had been in her care and were with one or two exceptions, full of affection and gratitude. One of the exceptions was a sheaf of correspondence between Glory and a boy called Mel. He was clearly angry and rebellious and one of his letters to Glory was full of hate and expressed in language that can only be described as disgusting. Glory's reply was impressively firm and calm, and Mel's response was a long letter of remorse and contrition which ended, 'Glory, I swear you are the best!'

As well as all the letters, there was a list of all the foster children Glory had looked after, together with photographs. Dan and Peggy searched through them to find Mel.

Peggy chuckled as she studied his face.

'He looks like a little angel!' she said.

When they had looked through everything in the file, Dan closed it and said, 'Well, what do you think, Peg?'

'I think she'd be great for the little Mulligans. I'd certainly trust any of my kids with her. But then I've known Glory for a long time. She doesn't live far from me, and I got to know her when we were both young mothers. She's one of those people who would do a good turn to anybody. When she first came to Barnham a lot of folk took against her, partly her colour, I suppose. There was more racism in those days. But also Glory was always one to speak out, she never hid her light under a bushel, and some of her neighbours resented that. But they soon grew to accept her, and now I doubt if there's anyone round our way that doesn't respect Glory.'

'She is an unusual woman, though, isn't she?' Dan said. 'And I'm not just talking about her clothes. She doesn't talk like someone from the Carribean – which I assume she comes from?'

'No, she talks like a lady, doesn't she? Glory came over from Barbados when she was five with her mother, to join her father who had a job on the railways, I think. But soon after they arrived, both parents were killed in an accident and Glory was put into Care. Then, after a year, she was adopted by a middle-class, professional family, and that's why she talks like she does.'

'I see. And knowing what it's like to be in Care will have given her the empathy she obviously has with her foster-children. Well, I agree with you, Peg. Except for her age, Glory seems the ideal foster mother for the Mulligan children.'

The people at Social Services agreed, but Kate Moriarty was not happy. 'They've just got used to us,' she said to Dan, 'surely it can't be right to move the poor things again. And has this Glory person had any experience with Downs?' 'She's had experience with just about anything you can think of, Kate,' said Dan.

'But if she's as big and black and old as you say, won't the children be frightened of her?'

'Kate,' said Dan, 'I'm sure this is the right decision. Ever since I've known you, I've worried that you take on too much, and you look exhausted. I'd like you to come and meet Glory. Then you can fill her in about the children and see how you feel after you've met her.'

As Dan knew they would, the two women hit it off right away, and when Glory left, Kate turned a smiling face to Dan. 'You were right, Dan, Glory's just great. I feel a lot happier now.'

He smiled back at her. 'Well, I hope you're also going to be a lot more sensible now, Mrs Moriarty!' he said. And after Kate left he spent some time musing on the two women, and what he saw as their sheer goodness.

CHAPTER TWENTY-ONE

As the months went by, Rupert put extra effort into his work, determined to do all he could for Dan in the relatively short time that was left. Once he even volunteered to do Dan's shift at the prison, which took a great deal of courage.

Somehow he and Imogen still found time to plan their wedding down to the smallest detail. Because of the sadness – and in a few cases anger too – felt at Rupert's leaving the priesthood (betraying his calling, as some put it), they had decided on a quiet wedding. Just family and a few close friends were invited.

To her delight, Peggy was one of them. Her first thought was 'What can I give them?' her second, 'What shall I wear?', and the third, 'What about all those people who would love to go but are not invited?'

It was this last anxiety that preoccupied her for some days. She went round to see Walter, who was beginning to make a real success of his business. He now owned three minibuses and had somehow managed to complete a business course in his spare time. He had turned his spare bedroom into an office, complete with all the latest technology.

He was not at all surprised by his mother's plan, and grateful that she didn't want him to drive three minibus loads of people to Yorkshire and back for nothing. 'Just charge them as little as you can, duck, without making a loss for yourself.'

Walter had no bookings for Easter Monday and he agreed to her request. He then used the internet to find the name and telephone number of the Royal Oak at

Appledown, and Peggy contacted the landlord, who agreed to provide sixty picnic lunches on the day of the wedding.

As Peggy walked home she felt very happy and grateful to her son. But at the same time she realised that the hardest part of her plan was yet to be tackled. She had to find sixty people who wanted to go to Rupert and Imogen's wedding and who could be safely sworn to secrecy; the secrecy worried her right up until the day the young couple left for Appledown. Only then did she confide in Dan. 'They won't mind, will they? I mean, I know it's a sort of gate-crashing, but Rupert's parents won't have to feed them and it will make everyone so happy.' Dan was delighted. 'Peggy, that's absolutely wonderful!' he said, 'as long as there will be nobody left behind who would have loved to go.'

'Well, I've done my best,' Peggy said, 'but the Drews and Amanda Trumpington have big cars and they've offered to take anyone like that.'

Dan stared at her. 'Peg, you're a genius!' he said, 'Oh, and I promise I won't let on!' 'You'd better not!' Peggy laughed.

There were no showers on the day of the April wedding and the sun shone warmly from a cloudless sky. Imogen wore a simple white dress and flowers in her hair. As she walked down the aisle on her father's arm she didn't register that the church was full of people: She looked steadily ahead to where Rupert was waiting for her. The vows, which bride and groom had written themselves, were spoken clearly enough for everyone to hear and it seemed that all the women – even Kate Moriarty, who reckoned to despise sentimentality – and even some of the men, had tears in their eyes.

It was only at the end, when Rupert and Imogen turned to walk back down the aisle, that the impact of sixty unexpected, smiling, clapping guests struck them. Eagerly invited by Imogen, Rupert and Rupert's parents, everybody trooped across the churchyard to the primrose-studded garden of the vicarage where trestle tables were set up to be laden with food for the reception. Rupert's mother was the only person looking worried, but Imogen touched her arm. 'It's all right, Hester, there's food coming from the Royal Oak.'

Old William O'Connor, sitting under a tree in his wheelchair said to Dan, 'I didn't know whether to come. But I'm very glad I did,' and echoing what everyone else present felt, he added, 'I'll never forget this day.'

CHAPTER TWENTY TWO

Dan had arranged to take his annual holiday directly after the wedding. He was going to Ireland, to stay with his mother in County Cork for a week. He was delighted when his Benedictine friend, Anselm, asked if he could come with him.

'That will be great,' Dan said, 'I'll enjoy your company, but I must warn you of one thing.'

'What's that?'

'Well, I'm afraid my old mother has a thing about the English. Quite simply, she doesn't like them. She's vowed never to set foot in England, and no amount of cajoling will persuade her to come and stay with me. But if you're willing to cope with her, I'd love to show you my beautiful birthplace!'

Anselm laughed. 'I look forward to it, Dan, all of it, and especially your mother.'

As it turned out, Mrs Spring was very happy to welcome them both. Well into her eighties, she was still sprightly in mind and body and she thoroughly enjoyed making huge meals for 'the boys', as she called them.

For a whole week, to their surprise, it didn't rain, and Anselm was enchanted by the coast of West Cork. And while Dan was renewing old acquaintances and reminiscing about his boyhood, Anselm explored the countryside. In the evenings, after a splendid meal with Dan's mother, they sat for a while by the peat fire, and then when she had slipped away to bed, they walked the mile to the village pub to enjoy the cheerful company, the beer and the singing. On their last night, Anselm was persuaded to sing a solo.

At the end of their visit they both looked relaxed and fit, if a trifle heavier. They said goodbye to Mrs Spring who warmly invited her son and his English friend to come again.

When they parted after the ferry crossing, Anselm said, 'I can never thank you enough for this holiday, Dan. It's just what I needed. Your mother is wonderful, and as for West Cork, well, it's just as I imagined, only more so!'

Anselm drove back to his monastery but Dan made his way to a cottage in mid-Wales where he had arranged to spend a few days alone, to pray and take stock of his situation. He spent a lot of time thinking about St Bon's, and especiaily about the people in his parish. He thought about his mistakes and failures. He wondered how the little Mulligan family were getting on with Glory, and he wondered how he would manage without Rupert. He knew he would miss him terribly, not only because his workload would heavily increase, but mainly because Rupert had become like a son or a younger brother.

But on the last day of his retreat Dan made a decision to become more positive. He tried to look at things from the people's point of view. What did they want from their parish? What did they need?

And he remembered how over the past months one or two people, people he particularly respected, like Bill Clough and Sister Julian and Robbie Moriarty, had come to him at different times asking him to open up St Bon's crypt. He recalled that he had undertaken to think about it, and realised that he had been so caught up with other concerns that he'd hardly listened to these good people.

So when he got back home to Barnham, he first gave Peggy, eagerly smiling in welcome, a huge hug, and then, before tackling his answer phone and emails, telephoned Bill Clough, Sister Julian and Robbie Moriarty and made an appointment to see them together to discuss the crypt.

Bill, who was an architect, came with rough plans already drawn up, Julian described her longing for a shelter for the homeless and Robbie outlined his ideas for a community centre, an attractive meeting place for all sorts of activities.

Their enthusiasm was infectious. Dan examined Bill's plans closely.

'It all looks and sounds wonderful,' he said, 'and of course I don't want to put a damper on it, but what about the ...'

The three of them were grinning at him.

'*Cost!*' they chorused.

Then Bill said, 'We knew you were bound to ask that, Dan, but while you were away the Finance Committee received a sizable legacy from Miss Glover. She left her whole estate to St Bon's! We've costed it all out as far as is realistic and possibie, and we reckon we could at least make a start. Moreover, Lydia Drew and Amanda Trumpington have undertaken to organise fund-raising. Apparently Amanda has considerable experience in this field and as you know, both ladies have just the right personal skills to succeed in something like this.' Then Sister Julian spoke. 'A number of people have offered their services for nothing. We've got a lawyer, an accountant and a builder, and lots of people have volunteered their skills in their spare time, painters, decorators, plumbers ...

'Hang on,' Dan said, 'am I dreaming all this? How on earth have you organised it all in the short time I've been away?'

'We haven't,' Robbie said, 'we've been working on it for over a year. Each of us, when we approached you, sensed that you had more than enough on your mind, so we decided to do some exploring and find out how feasible our ideas are.'

'This is fantastic,' said Dan. 'You can certainly count me in. When can we get started?'

They got started at the end of May. Dan made a few affempts to join in the work with various parishioners, chiefly acting as a sort of decorator's mate, but everyone seemed to understand that his time was limited. More than once a parishioner said to him: 'Leave it to us, Father. You've got better things to do.'

He couldn't help wondering if what they really meant was, 'You're only getting in the way!' So the months went by and the work went on and Dan's days were as exhausting and as stimulating as ever.

CHAPTER TWENTY-THREE

In October, Year Six at St Boniface's Primary School sent Dan an invitation to their Harvest Festival. He always loved visiting the school and he was conscious that it was some time since his last visit. He didn't go regularly, having uncomfortable memories of his own childhood when the local priest, who had little knowledge of children and none of teaching, would waste hours of lesson time speaking about things they couldn't possibly understand.

As far as he could, Dan liked to get to know the children through their families. He was pleased to see that the invitation did not include a request for him to speak, and he was interested in meeting a new music teacher one or two people had told him about.

The school was bright and full of colour. Paintings by the children decorated the walls, and fruit and vegetables and other produce filled every shelf and spare corner. Dan gave his contribution, a fruit cake made by Peggy, to Johnny Mulligan, who was one of the children receiving the gifts. He saw Helen Drew arrive with a box of iced cakes and old Oliver Hardy staggering under the weight of a giant marrow.

Dan was led by the headmaster, Sidney Porter, to a seat in the front row, but he declined it, saying he didn't want to block the view of the children behind him. Instead he sat at the back with the parents and grandparents.

At two o'clock promptly, the children's choir who had been sitting on the stage stood up. The audience of children and adults fell silent. Then a young man Dan hadn't seen before stepped in front and one of the teachers, Myra

Hunt, slipped quietly over to the piano and the young man raised his arm. The children were all focused on him and as the music began they started to sing.

Dan felt the hairs on the back of his neck stand up. The hymn was one he knew, 'For the beauty of the earth' with the tune by John Rutter, but he had never heard a group of children sing like this. During the afternoon there were other songs, sometimes by the choir, and sometimes by the whole school. At the end there was no address; only a silent tableau.

After a few moments, a table was carried to the front of the stage. Four children came and sat at one end. They were eating chocolate biscuits, cake and ice cream and drinking lemonade with obvious relish. Opposite them, four other children were standing. They had nothing to eat or drink and they stared miserably at the others. Sometimes they reached out their hands towards the children who were eating, but these either ignored them or shook their heads then, after a few minutes, one of the hungry children crept towards the others with his hand outstretched, and one of the eaters gave him a small cake. He immediately took it back to the others and broke it into four pieces and shared it with them. The others carried on eating and the hungry ones continued in vain to hope. No words were spoken. That was all. Then the eight children went quietly back to their places and the choir began to sing softly.

When it was all over, the parents were given tea and biscuits and all the goodies were packed up ready to be taken to the hospital and the Salvation Army. Dan went over to the young man. 'Hullo,' he said, 'I'm Dan, Father Daniel Spring.' The young man smiled. 'Oh, I'm glad to meet you, Father. I'm Stephen, Stephen Wykes. I've been to Mass at St Bon's and I love it. It's a wonderful parish.'

'Why, thanks,' said Dan, 'but I don't think we've met before?'

'No, I always have to leave early. I catch the bus to go over to see my mother every Sunday. But we're hoping to find a flat for her here in Barnham which will make life a whole lot easier for both of us.'

Dan congratulated Stephen warmly on the children's singing, but then Bill Clough politely interrupted to say he needed to talk about the crypt. When Dan turned back to continue his conversation with Stephen, he had disappeared.

CHAPTER TWENTY-FOUR

Dan didn't see Stephen for a couple of weeks, but in the meantime he had been thinking about the young man and his talent. He had been impressed not only by Stephen's obvious musical ability, but by his relationship with the children, friendly but firm. Then one Sunday after Mass, when he was standing by the door as usual to greet the parishioners and be available to them if they needed to see him, Stephen came up to him with a pleasant-faced middle-aged woman. 'This is my mother, Father,' he said. The woman smiled and held out her hand. 'I'm Susan Wykes', she said, 'and we're so excited. I've bought a flat! We exchanged contracts last week and yesterday Stephen helped me to decide on curtains and carpets and things like that. I can't wait to be settled but he insists on decorating it first!'

'Well, Mum, you have to admit that you'd find it hard to live with the gloomy colours the flat is painted with now!'

Dan laughed. 'You're very welcome, Mrs Wykes, Susan,' he said, 'and I hope you'll be very happy here. But I must introduce you to some people.' He caught hold of Lydia Drew's sleeve as she was passing, and drew her towards Stephen and his mother, at the same time catching Agnes Greenwood's eye and beckoning her over.

'Lydia, Agnes,' he said, this is Susan Wykes, she's Stephen's mother – you may know Stephen teaches at St Boniface's. Anyway, she's coming to live in the parish and doesn't know anyone yet. Would you have time to take her for coffee?'

It was actually quite inconvenient for both Lydia and

Agnes, but they were too polite to refuse. As they walked towards the sacristy where until the new crypt was ready, coffee was served, Dan called Stephen back. 'There's something, well, frankly two things I'd like to ask you about,' he said. 'Could you come round to the presbytery one day after school?' 'Yes, surely,' Stephen answered, 'tomorrow, if that suits you?'

Stephen arrived at four o'clock on Monday and Dan had tea and Peggy's chocolate cake ready for him. 'I'm hoping you haven't been here long enough to have all your free time booked,' said Dan.

'Well, no, I'm still finding my feet. Why, have you something you would like me to do?'

'Yes, I have. In fact two things. But I don't want to make unfair demands on you, Stephen. I know teachers have a heavy workload these days. So don't let me pressure you into anything.'

Stephen laughed. He felt at at ease with this man. 'You're getting me worried now,' he said, 'what superhuman tasks are you going to demand of me, Father?'

'Everyone, well nearly everyone, calls me Dan. I prefer it. Well, the first superhuman task is this: Do you think you could muster, and teach and regularly conduct a children's choir for the church?'

'Wow! That's not a task, that would be a pleasure! I'd love to!'

'Great!' Dan caught Stephen's enthusiasm. Then he said, 'The other thing might be more daunting. Rupert, the young priest who left to get married in April, used to be a presence at the Youth Club. They're good kids, on the whole, and they seem to be managing very well without an adult, but I simply don't have the time.'

Stephen interrupted. 'I can't say "I'd love to" because I have no experience of teenagers. But I'd certainly like to try. How would you feel, though, Father Dan, if my partner came along too?'

'That would be fine,' Dan said, 'Does she …?'

'He,' corrected Stephen. Dan tried hard to conceal his surprise, and failed. He rallied, 'Does he have any experience of working with teenagers?'

'Oh, yes, Eddie is a qualified youth worker, but he hasn't been able to get a job in Barnham yet. He'd love the experience and I can promise you the kids will take to him.'

'Well, that sounds ideal,' Dan said. 'I'd like to meet Eddie. Maybe you'd both like to come round to supper any day next week?'

CHAPTER TWENTY-FIVE

Thanks to Stephen and Eddie everything seemed to be going very well with both the choir and the Youth Group. Dan met Basher in the street one afternoon. 'Hey, man!' Basher greeted him. 'We owe you. It was you had the idea to send us Steve and Eddie, yeah?'

'I suppose it was, Basher. Are they settling in all right then?'

'Man, you should come along and see. We're doing all sorts of sports now, organised and proper. That's down to Ed. An' we're doin' the discussions again, what Rupert started. We'd sort of let that go a bit. But the best, for me anyway, is Steve. Man, we've got a band, a real band, an' I'm the drummer. You watch this space, Farver, an' you might get a surprise after Christmas. Let's say, put Twelfth Night in your diary, fingers crossed!' Basher beamed down on Dan. 'I guarantee you'll enjoy it, man!'

Dan was delighted with this encounter and possibly happier still when Stephen invited him to a choir rehearsal at the beginning of December. The choir were due to sing for the first time in public and there was to be a Festival of Nine Lessons and Carols with a difference. Stephen told Dan that Eddie, together with Sister Lucy from the convent, had chosen the readings, and only a few of them were from scripture. 'They're all appropriate, though, Dan.' Lucy had assured him. 'Some of them are beautiful and one is funny. Eddie has a way with words and he wrote one of them himself.'

But when Dan went into the church for the rehearsal, a child was singing a solo, the first verse of the traditional

'Once in Royal David's City' and Dan stood still, struck by the purity and beauty of the boy's voice. When the verse was over, Dan slipped into a pew. He saw that the boy was Michael Foster. Looking at him, Dan thought, 'This can't be real. He sings like an angel, he even looks like an angel!' Michael was small for his age. His hair was fair and his eyes blue.

Dan thoroughly enjoyed the rest of the rehearsal, and particularly liked the readings chosen by Eddie and Lucy. As he walked home he congratulated himself. For once you've done something right, Daniel Spring, he told himself. Stephen and Eddie are a great asset and already they're making such a difference in the parish, especially for the youngsters.

But in a very short time he was ruefully to recall the old adage 'Pride comes before a fall.' As he arrived home he saw that someone was ringing his doorbell.

'Hello,' he called, 'it's me, Father Dan.' The figure turned round. It was a woman. He recognised her then. It was Wendy Foster, the mother of Michael, someone he knew quite well. He hurried up to her, eager to share his delight in Michael. But before he could speak, she said in an unmistakably cold voice, 'Good evening, Father. May I come in? There's something I must tell you.'

Once inside the house, Wendy agreed to take off her coat and sit down but refused Dan's offer of refreshment.

'I've come to tell you that I'm taking Michael out of the choir at once and William out of the Youth Group.' Before Dan could say anything she continued, her voice rising. 'How could you, how could you, Father, let those people near my boys? They're so innocent and vulnerable and I, we, (Dennis agrees with me), we simply don't understand how you could do something so outrageous!'

Dan was completely flummoxed. He couldn't understand what on earth the woman was on about.

'I'm sorry, Wendy, but I honestly don't understand!

What is it that's upsetting you?'

'Upsetting me? Huh, is that what you think, Father? Well, let me tell you, I'm not upset, I'm absolutely horrified and disgusted.'

'But I don't understand. What have I done?'

'What have you done? You mean you really don't know? Well, I'll tell you, you've let loose not one but two paedophiles to do whatever they want with my boys. It's not just wrong, it's evil. These men are evil, and you are evil to give them that freedom!'

Dan was astonished for a few seconds and then he became conscious of the anger mounting within him, anger that he knew would exceed Wendy's if he couldn't control it. Silently he whispered a prayer, a prayer for calm and compassion on this silly woman. Then he took a deep breath.

'Wendy,' he said, 'I'm afraid you've completely misunderstood the situation and these two young men. It's true that Stephen and Eddie are gay, but it's a terrible mistake to equate homosexuality with paedophilia. These boys are no more paedophiles than you or I. And let me tell you, Wendy, neither of them is remotely evil. Both are a great force for good in the parish, and I hope you can bring yourself to feel grateful to them for what they're doing for your sons.'

He paused and Wendy said nothing. So he went on, 'I don't know whether you know it, but your Michael has the most beautiful voice I've ever heard in a child.'

But Wendy didn't answer him. She got to her feet and he fetched her coat.

At the front door she turned and said, 'You used the word 'gay' to describe these people. I hate that. They are anything but gay in the true sense of the word!'

Dan made himself speak gently. 'Actually, gay is an acronym. Do you know what the letters stand for?'

'No, and I don't want to know,' she said curtly. She was out of the door, but Dan called after her, G A Y – good as you!' he called.

Then as soon as he was indoors again, he put his head in his hands. 'Oh, God, I handled that so badly,' he prayed, 'and that bit of point scoring at the end was pathetic and childish.'

He blamed himself, but he also wondered how an intelligent woman like Wendy Foster could have such a blind spot.

Michael duly left the choir and William the Youth Group. When Stephen asked Dan if he knew why, the priest hesitated. That was enough for Stephen. He smiled. 'Don't worry, it happens all the time,' he said. 'I expect Mrs Foster heard I was gay and assumed I am a paedophile.'

'Well, yes,' Dan was surprised at the young man's calm. 'But aren't you angry?'

'No, I'm used to it. Don't worry. But I *am* disappointed. Young Michael's voice is exceptional. But as you know, Father, these things sometimes turn out for the best. I know I won't find anyone with a purer, sweeter voice, but well, we'll have to see what happens.'

CHAPTER TWENTY-SIX

It was a happy Christmas, the best that Dan could remember. The main room in the new crypt was ready in time. Bill Clough and his band of builders had finished their work there and a host of volunteers had painted and decorated and cleaned it. Lydia Drew and Kate Moriarty had joined together to organise a Christmas dinner in the crypt for the homeless and the lonely. Dan stood behind a table handing out slices of turkey – his feet were aching and he was ravenously hungry, but the atmosphere in the crypt was wonderful. 'I wouldn't exchange this for anything,' he confided to Hilary Clough who was ladling gravy next to him.

'Nor me,' she said. And he remembered it might be Hilary's last Christmas.

In the afternoon the primary school put on a musical Christmas play in the church, produced by Stephen Wykes. Dan had seen hundreds of nativity plays but he found this one specially moving. Ella Broughton, a spina bifida in a wheelchair, took the part of the Virgin Mary, and little Tommy White was a king. Unfortunately his magnificent gold head-dress fell off as he was presenting the frankincense to the infant Jesus and his bell-like tones rang out through the church: 'I've dropped me bloody crown!'

There was spontaneous laughter in the congregation and Dan found himself nervously looking round for Daphne Pollard, the most prudish of his parishioners, but he couldn't see her. The singing and the percussion band brought the play to a triumphant finish. Dan was very tired when he got home. He indulged in a Christmas nightcap, happily going over the events of the day. It had been a marvellous Christmas, thanks to his wonderful parishioners. In this euphoric state he said his prayers, got himself to bed and fell instantly asleep.

Boxing Day was different. It was raining and there was a cold raw wind. Only a handful of his wonderful parishioners turned up for the ten o'clock Mass. Dan went back to the presbytery feeling sadly deflated. He had told Peggy not to come in; he had declined the invitations of various people to share their festivities because he felt it would be wrong to favour one family rather than another. He had hesitated when the Sisters from the convent invited him to lunch. They worked very hard in the parish and he was particularly grateful to Sister Julian who despite her age and infirmity was tireless in visiting the sick and the lonely. Also, he knew he would have enjoyed Lucy's company. But in the end he thanked them and said 'No,' thinking that perhaps they would really prefer to relax in their own community for the short break.

He looked in the fridge. There was some cold turkey and a piece of cold Christmas pudding. Maybe I'm over-tired, he thought. He couldn't summon the energy to heat the food or prepare any vegetables. He ate the meal without enjoyment and switched on the television but there was nothing to interest him. He went into the chapel and tried to pray but he just fell empty and low.

He was as always honest before God.

'The plain truth is, Lord, I'm lonely.' He thought of the previous Christmas, spent with Rupert. They hadn't done anything special on Boxing Day. It had been cold and sunny, he remembered, and they'd gone for a long bracing walk. Rupert had cooked a delicious supper and they'd had a companionable evening by the fire.

There's no point in lighting the fire just for one, he thought, and then shook himself. 'What a load of miserable self-pity!' he chided himself. 'Daniel Spring, you've got hundreds of friends, you don't know what loneliness is! How about the really lonely people? What's it like for them?'

Into is mind came a picture of Daphne Pollard. He hadn't seen her all over Christmas, except at the quiet early morning Mass on Christmas Day, and she must have slipped out before he got to the porch to greet people. Poor old Daphne! What sort of Christmas can she be having? he wondered.

He put on his warmest clothing, and set out briskly for Daphne's flat.

CHAPTER TWENTY-SEVEN

Daphne was alone. She had been alone all Christmas. She never went to Midnight Mass because once some drunks had come in straight from the pub and ruined it for everybody. She didn't go to help with the Christmas dinner in the crypt because she disapproved of lay-abouts, tramps and cadgers. And she didn't go to the nativity play because she didn't like children.

Daphne hated Christmas. She often felt desperately lonely, but never so much as at this time of year. On Boxing Day the afternoon and evening stretched endlessly ahead – what was there to do? She tried the television, but seeing more jollification she hastily switched it off.

Well – she shrugged her shoulders – there's nothing else for it. With a gleam in her eye she went to her bedroom, opened a drawer and pulled out a woollen jumper. Underneath was her guilty secret, a pile of romantic novels. She selected one called *The Price of Passion* and took it into the living room. There she put on one bar of her electric fire, wrapped a rug round her knees and opened a small box of chocolates which she had bought for herself as a Christmas treat.

She settled down to enjoy a good read. The story's heroine was called Viola – she was twenty-one and had wide-apart violet eyes and a rose-bud mouth; but nevertheless, Daphne, colourless, plain and middle-aged, managed to identify with her in her longings and dreams.

It was only on the last page that the hero revealed his passionate love for Viola. Daphne threw down the book and burst into loud sobbing. It was always the same – the happy ending, the dream fulfilled – but never for her. It never had been and never would.

She was filled now with self-disgust. How could she read such rubbish? And she'd finished the box of chocolates – that was gluttony. Tears coursed down her sallow face, soaking the top of her jumper, and she made no effort to stop the flow. She knew from frequent experience that there would be at least some measure of release in this crying.

Then the doorbell rang. Frantically Daphne kicked *The Price of Passion* behind the sofa, frantically she mopped up her tears. Who on earth could it be? No-one ever called.

It was Father Dan.

She was surprised, pleased, suspicious, (what could he want?) and panicky, (what can I give him? I've finished the chocolates!)

She led him into the cheerless room. Dan shivered involuntarily. It was spotlessly clean but drab and comfortless.

'Please sit down, Father,' said Daphne. 'Can I get you a cup of tea?'

He looked at her closely and spoke spontaneously. 'Daphne, you've been crying!' He put out his hand and touched her gently on the shoulder.

She sprang back. And screamed at him. 'Don't touch me! How dare you! Just because you're a priest you think you can come poking into my private life! Well, you can't. Of course I haven't been crying – I've just got a cold, that's all.'

Dan was looking at her, but she didn't see the compassion in his eyes and she broke down again, sobbing and weeping.

'You don't understand!' she shouted. 'You don't know how it is. Everyone likes you – you've got hundreds of friends and admirers. But nobody likes me. I'm so lonely, Father, so desperately lonely!'

She sat down, shoulders hunched, head bent forward,

rocking herself as her tears splashed down on to her lap. Dan, forgetting her first outburst in his anxiety to comfort her, put his arm round her shoulder. Immediately she reared up, glaring at him.

'Don't touch me! I told you! Now go away. I don't want you here!'

Dan went. It was half-past five and quite dark. He began to walk aimlessly round the town, angry with himself. 'You're a failure, Dan Spring,' he said to himself. 'You seem to be successful, and Daphne's right, you're so popular, but when it comes to the crunch you're no good. How you enjoyed being fairy godfather to the little Mulligans, and doling out Christmas dinners to the homeless! It made you feel good, didn't it? And all the time you never gave a thought to a faithful parishioner like Daphne, you didn't even realise how unhappy she is, and when you finally got to visit her you just couldn't cope. Father Daniel Spring –huh – what a fraud! What a sham!'

CHAPTER TWENTY-EIGHT

He thought of the evening ahead and his heart sank. What would he do? What would he have for supper? I suppose I could boil myself an egg, he thought glumly.

He found he was in a little back street he didn't know. He glanced up at the name: Rowan Terrace. Of course there wasn't a rowan tree in sight. The terraced houses fronted the street. As he passed them he peered in some of the windows. The front rooms he saw looked cosy and bright. In one a small child was playing by a Christmas tree, in another an old couple sat watching television and laughing. Dan's misery increased. In spite of all his self-castigating he was intensely aware of his own loneliness.

Then, across the street, he saw a window different from the others. There was a single candle lit in the window. He crossed over. In this house the wall dividing two small rooms had been knocked down and he was looking into a room that surprised him. One wall was entirely lined with books and there was a spinning wheel beside the open fire. It looked friendly and welcoming.

He glanced at the door and saw that it was number seventeen. 17 Rowan Terrace. He knew that address – it must be on one of the many lists he had filed away in his study. But which one of his parishioners lived there?

Dan hesitated. His experience with Daphne had hardly encouraged him. After a quick prayer for courage he knocked on the door. In a moment it was opened – by Agnes Greenwood.

Dan was astonished and very pleased. Agnes was smiling, obviously delighted to see him. 'Come in, Dan, come in quickly out of the cold,' she said. 'How lovely to see you!'

The warmth of the room welcomed him and he sat gratefully in a comfortable chair by the fire.

'I haven't any alcohol, I'm afraid,' said Agnes, 'I can't afford it any more, but will you have supper with me?' She clapped her hands like a little girl. 'Oh, do say Yes, Dan, please. You see I treated myself to half a dozen free range eggs – it was my Christmas present to myself. I was just going to boil one for my supper. Won't you have one too?' 'Well, thank you, I'd love to,' said Dan. He felt a bit guilty thinking of his own Christmas presents to himself – a new television set and a giant bottle of whiskey. He didn't much care for boiled eggs, but …

In the event, it was a perfect meal. The brown speckled eggs were exactly as he liked them, the toast was hot and buttery, and afterwards there was a fresh fruit salad.

He helped Agnes to wash up and wondered about her. He had never realised that she hadn't much money, never thought of visiting her. Dan loved visiting but only went to see the old, the housebound and the sick. They sat on either side of the fire talking of Christmas and then of Hilary Clough.

'She's taking it so well,' said Agnes. 'I can't believe she's going to die so soon. She's wonderful. She has such a strong faith and trust in God. And she's been such a good friend to me.' She laughed self-consciously. 'Practically all my clothes are Hilary's castoffs.'

Dan looked at her. He had always thought of her as someone peaceful, strong, immensely kind. But he realised he had never really looked at her or thought about her. She was tall and graceful, and the dress of soft green wool that had been Hilary's suited her. Her face was deeply lined and her hair quite grey, but her fine bone structure and bright grey eyes made her attractive. He glanced round the room and noticed the picture over the fireplace. It was a large framed print of The Prodigal Son with his father and brother. Dan loved his own print of this story, by Rembrandt, which had pride of place in his bedroom, but this one was quite different. For a long time Dan gazed at the faces of the son and his father, moved by the intensity of the remorse and compassion. Agnes saw him, 'It's beautiful, isn't it? It's by Sieger Koder and for me it encapsulates everything our faith is about: forgiveness and love.' Dan glanced at the other figure, the older son. Am I like him? he wondered sadly.

There was a silence between them. How strange, thought Dan, I know her so little and yet I feel completely at ease with her.

'You don't seem your usual self tonight, Dan,' said Agnes. 'You look a bit better now but when I opened the door you looked dreadful. Is there anything troubling you?'

Suddenly, without warning, the tears came. She let him cry, saying nothing, doing nothing except hand him a tissue. After a while he told her about Daphne and his disgust with himself.

Agnes listened attentively, and when he finished speaking said, 'It's good, isn't it?'

'Good?' echoed Dan, surprised.

'Yes, it's good that you found out about Daphne. We can now try to do something about her. And it's good that you've had the chance to find out something about yourself, isn't it?'

'Well, yes' Dan said slowly. 'And it's especially good to have friends like you.' Then he laughed. 'I haven't cried in years. Thank you, Agnes, thanks for everything.'

CHAPTER TWENTY-NINE

One afternoon early in January, Kate Moriarty came to see Dan. Whenever Kate arrived he was always a little wary, wondering what she would be coming up with next.

'I've come about the homeless, Dan. The night shelter in the crypt is doing fine. People are very generous about giving food and manning it at night, but it's just not big enough. I was there last night and we had to turn away five people.'

'Oh Lord! I am sorry,' said Dan. 'Where would they have gone, do you know?'

'Oh yes, I know all right. They slept in the cattle market. It was snowing and it's Christmas time and that's the best our town can do for them!'

'What do you want me to do?' asked Dan.

'Well, we've got a lot of signatures already, people have been going round this morning collecting them. And I've made an appointment to see the Housing Manager at the Council Offices on Thursday, the day after tomorrow. I'm hoping as many people as possible will turn up in support. Can you rally the parishioners?'

'Not easily as there won't be a Sunday Mass before the meeting,' said Dan thoughtfully, 'but I'll spread the word as much as I can and you can count on me to be there.'

'Thanks a lot, Dan.' Kate was no time-waster, and she left briskly.

On Thursday morning Dan woke with a splitting headache and aching limbs. He managed to get through Mass and then crawled back to bed, setting his alarm for twelve noon. When it rang, the effort of getting out of bed was almost too much. He was shivering as he pulled on his clothes. Luckily the council offices were only half a mile away. It was snowing and there weren't many people about, but at the offices a group of about thirty had gathered. A reporter and photographer were there.

Dan scarcely took in what was happening. Suddenly Kate took him by the arm and said, 'Come on, Dan. We want you in the front of the picture – to lend a note of respectability.'

Numbly, Dan did as he was told. Then people began to move away and he turned to follow them, aware of dizziness. Someone seized his arm firmly and he heard the unmistakeable voice of Connie Brown.

'Father, you're not well. Come over here and sit down while I call a taxi.' He let her lead him to a chair and after that he remembered nothing until he opened his eyes to find Peggy's anxious face bending over him. He was in bed.

The doctor told him to stay in bed for a week and Peggy made sure that he did, bringing him drinks every two hours and generally cosseting him. She kept all visitors at bay until the fifth day when Sir Reginald Froggett arrived and demanded to see Father Spring.

'I'll just see if he is well enough,' said Peggy. She found the man irritatingly pompous. But Sir Reginald brushed her aside and made his way upstairs. Reluctantly Peggy followed him and when he was trying to find Dan's room she led him up to the attic.

'Father,' he said, without preamble, 'I've come to register my annoyance. Just look at this!' He produced a copy of the local paper and showed Dan a photograph of the protesters at the council offices. There was Dan on the front row looking extremely foolish, Dan felt.

'It's a disgrace! It's all wrong!' Sir Reginald shouted. 'A priest's job is to preach and administer the sacraments, not to meddle in politics. Mildred is shocked and so am I. I'm sorry but we've decide to vote with our feet. We won't be coming to St Boniface's anymore!'

'Well, that's a relief!' Peggy, who was standing by the door spoke hotly. As the old man turned round she went on, 'And don't you ask Father Dan to explain his actions. He's not well enough and I'll answer for him.'

Dan lay there, staring at Peggy, astonished. He had no idea she was capable of this. And as she continued he was even more amazed.

'Have you forgotten, Sir Reginald,' she went on, 'that Our Lord came to set the downtrodden free, that he loved the poor, that he said "Whatever you do to the least of my brothers, you do unto me"?'

Sir Reginald stared at her for a moment, then bowed curtly and made his way out of the house. 'Phew!' said Dan. And as soon as they heard the front door slam, they both burst out laughing. 'That's done me so much good, Peggy – you were wonderful!' said Dan at last. 'I feel ready to cope with visitors now. And please will you ask Connie Brown to come to see me – I've always found her rather a trial – though nothing like Sir Reggie, of course. But I owe her a lot and I want to thank her properly.'

CHAPTER THIRTY

The day after he got up, his first visitor was Lydia Drew. She looked, as always, elegant and confident. She had brought flowers and a box of expensive chocolates. After the usual courtesies she said, 'Father, I've come on behalf of my Abigail. You know she's a bit of a harum-scarum, but she's a darling. I told you at the time, she was married in a Registry Office, but Justin is absolutely charming and now they've got the sweetest little baby, Arabella. Isn't that delightful?'

'Well, Abigail went to the priest to arrange the baptism, and do you know, the old fuddy-duddy refused to do it! Can you believe it? Anyway, I told Abbie not to worry. I explained that you are so understanding and tolerant and I said I knew you'd love to baptise Arabella. I just came to see when it would suit you.'

Dan smiled sadly and shook his head. 'Do Abigail and Justin practise their faith?' he asked.

'Well – no, well you know what young people are like nowadays, Father. She thinks we're all rather ridiculous. Abbie's always been so refreshingly honest, you know. She says she and Justin don't need God.'

'Why does she want the baby baptised, then?'

'I asked her that,' said Lydia. 'She said Justin's mother has this super christening robe that's been in the family for generations, and it's a good excuse for a party.'

'Lydia,' said Dan quite sharply, 'you're not thinking very clearly, are you? Do you think it would be fair to Arabella to baptise her if she's not going to be brought up as a Christian?'

Lydia looked at him wide-eyed. 'Father Dan, surely you're not going to refuse! Why, I was counting on you ...'

'You're a good woman, Lydia,' said Dan, 'and you've done a great deal in this parish. And I know Abigail is lovely. But she's not a committed Christian, is she? Not a Christian of any sort? Do ask her to come and see me if she'd like to, but at the moment I have to agree with her local fuddy-duddy priest. I'm not prepared to baptise Arabella.'

As Lydia was leaving, Daphne Pollard arrived. Dan watched with amusement as the two women greeted each other with smiles. Daphne had changed almost beyond recognition. Prompted by Agnes Greenwood, Lydia had taken Agnes under her wing and got her involved in various parish activities. She had even joined the charismatic prayer group. Now she smiled at Dan and said, 'I won't waste your time, Father, I just thought you'd like to know that Hilary is sinking fast.'

'Hilary Clough?' asked Dan, 'Oh dear, I didn't realise she was as bad as that.'

'It happened when you were ill, Father. I'm very fond of Hilary and Bill and I've been round there quite a bit. They're very good to me.'

'I dare say you're very good to them, Daphne, but you look worn out. Where were you last night?'

'Well, poor Bill was exhausted. I offered to stay up with Hilary,' Daphne said shyly. 'Do you think you could come round, Father, soon?'

'I'll come right away,' said Dan, and knowing he was taking a risk he put his arm round her shoulder in a gesture of affection. He felt her stiffen, but she didn't react as she had done at Christmas.

Two hours later, Hilary died peacefully. Bill was holding her hand, Dan and Daphne were kneeling by the bed.

It was Daphne who spoke first. 'I believe she is already with God,' she said.

CHAPTER THIRTY-ONE

As soon as Hilary had learnt about her cancer, she had re-signed from the Parish Council and Wilfrid Drew had taken her place. He turned out to be a great asset in that he was hard-working and efficient and willing to be involved in almost all of the council's work. He took his position very seriously, sometimes a little too seriously, Norah McGinty thought.

'He never knows when to leave well alone,' she confided to Peggy.

When Wilfrid heard that the bishop was coming to cele-brate Mass in the parish for the Feast of the Annunciation, he lost no time in going round to see Dan.

'We've got to be sure everything's ship-shape,' he said.

'How do you mean?' Dan was puzzled.

'Well, it's important to make a good impression,' and before Dan could respond to this he went on, 'So I've made some notes.' Dan suppressed a sigh and led the way into his study. He quickly cleared some space on his desk and both men sat down.

'First of all,' Wilfrid began, 'we've got to be sure that old Nelson O'Grady, and all traces of him, are out of the church the night before.'

'No,' said Dan, 'I could never agree to that, Wilfrid. That bench in the back corner of St Bon's is the only home Nelson's got. We can't possibly turn him out. Anyway he's a fixture, he's always there for Mass. What have you got against the poor chap?'

'Well, he's filthy, for a start. And his smell – it's disgust-ing. What if the bishop caught a whiff of that?'

Dan laughed. 'You don't need to worry about that. The bishop came out to Ecuador and spent a few weeks with me and I can assure you he encountered far worse smells in some places there than you could ever get with Nelson!'

Wilfrid saw that he would have to give in on that one. But now he produced a formidable-looking file.

'These are the various rotas,' he said. 'I made copies of them all for you, Father.' He handed Dan a sheaf of papers.

'I've marked on each one the person I thought would be best for the Annunciation Mass,' he said, 'but of course I realise you may like to change some of them.'

'But I don't understand,' Dan said, 'What's wrong with the way the rotas were already fixed for that day?'

Now it was Wilfrid's turn to laugh.

'What's wrong?' he said, 'Why almost everything! For instance, as the rotas stand, Norah McGinty is down to do the second reading, and you know, Father, she stumbles over the words – I'm not sure if it's her eyesight or maybe she's barely literate, but obviously we'll have to have someone else doing the second reading.' Before Dan could comment, Wilfrid went on. 'And then there's the offertory procession. The names down for the 25th March are Charles and Martha Simpson. I don't even know them but I'm told they're a couple in their seventies. Obviously it's not a good idea to have them shuffling up the aisle.'

Dan was laughing again. 'Oh, Wilfrid, you should get to know Charles and Martha. They may be in their seventies, but they think nothing of walking ten miles in a day. But seriously, I don't want you to waste any more of your time. I can see that you've been very thorough in preparing all this and I'm grateful as always for the way you put your heart and soul into things. But before you make any more suggestions, I want to make it clear that I don't want any of the rotas changed. We are not aiming to make a good impression. Do the rest of the parish council think as you do about this?'

'Well, I haven't actually discussed it with them yet ...'

'Right. Well, Wilfrid, if the parish council as a whole want me to go along with your ideas, I'm prepared to listen. But the bishop isn't coming to examine us, or give us a score for good conduct, and I strongly believe he should see us as we are, Nelson, Norah, the Simpsons, you and me, Wilfrid.'

He paused, seeing the man's crestfallen expression. 'I wish I were half as thorough and efficient and' – he glanced ruefully at his desk – 'as tidy as you, Wilfrid. And how about some coffee?'

Wilfrid was very disappointed. As he waited for Dan to bring in the coffee he thought, 'I've had to give in on every single point!'

But when Dan came back, he said, 'Just one more thing, Father. Please tell me we won't have that dreadful band from the Youth Club. The noise they make is deafening and I don't know any of their songs. Please say we won't have them caterwauling when the Bishop comes. In any case some of them aren't even Catholics!'

But Dan only smiled.

CHAPTER THIRTY-TWO

Dan felt a little guilty after Wilfrid had left. The bishop had been his good friend over a number of years, and he didn't feel the need to impress him. But of course it wasn't the same for Wilfrid. He was only doing the best he could for the parish. I shouldn't have trampled on all his ideas, Dan thought, silly though they were.

In the event, things ran fairly smoothly, and the impression the bishop received was of a happy, lively parish community. He particularly liked the Youth Club Band and made a mental note to talk to them afterwards.

Some people were disappointed when Dan got up to preach, because they were looking forward to hearing the bishop. But Dan began by explaining, 'Bishop John has asked me to preach today, because he wants to observe things just as they are, warts and all. But don't worry, he's going to talk to us at the end of Mass.'

'I'm going to say a few words about the Annunciation. For centuries this was kept as a feast of Our Lady, and in some places it is still known as Lady Day. This was to honour Mary, and her courage and humility when she submitted to God's will and agreed to become the mother of God's son.

'But the true title of this feast is The Annunciation of Our Lord, because it was on this day that God became a human being. For me it is, after Easter, the greatest feast of the church's year, because the day celebrates that moment when our God entered our world.

'It is the feast of Jesus, the feast of humanity, because he, Jesus, is not just one like us, but one *with* us. In my job, as your priest, I am privileged to meet all sorts of conditions of people: happy and sad, rich and poor, young and old, and many of you allow me to share your lives, your griefs and joys, your anxieties and hopes and failures and dreams. And I am very conscious, especially on this day, that in a way far more wonderful and powerful than I could begin to try to do, Jesus is with us, he who knows what it is to be truly human, who is there at the heart of our suffering, whatever form it takes, Jesus who will be with us, even to the end of time.'

At the end of Mass, before he blessed the people, the bishop went to stand on the sanctuary steps where Dan had stood to preach. He said, 'Thank you for having me here with you today. I haven't been to St Boniface's for a long time and I always love coming here. I think I used to come because I loved the building: it is older, much older and much more beautiful than most Catholic churches. But now I like coming because of you, the people. You seem like a real community, and you seem not just content, but really happy to meet together like this to celebrate Mass.

'I congratulate you on the shining brass and the lovely flowers, on the dignity of the young altar servers, on the way your readers had clearly prepared their scripture. As for the homily, well I have known Father Dan for a long time, and I've always admired his sermons. I remember once when we were both much younger and before I was made a bishop, I asked him once "How many hours do you spend writing your sermons?" and he said, "None. I don't write it. I just wait for the Holy Spirit to inspire me and she has never let me down so far!" I believe only a truly prayerful man could say that.

And lastly, could I ask you all, please, to come and join me in your splendid new crypt where there will be tea and coffee, and if I'm not mistaken, some delicious home-made goodies!' Smiling, he was about to step down, when he spoke again.

'I nearly forgot, but I did want to say that I am impressed, no, that's too feeble a word, I am excited by your Youth Club's brilliant band. I fancy myself as something of a drummer, but I'm nowhere near your standard', he looked across at Basher, smiling, and began to clap. The congregation joined in, not sure whom they were applauding, and not caring.

CHAPTER THIRTY-THREE

One evening Dan decided to walk round to the Youth Club. It was a long time since he had spent an evening with them and he enjoyed it. Quite a few of the young people came over to talk to him, some he knew well, others he guessed were not Catholics as he hadn't seen them before. The young guitarist, Tony, was sitting with him towards the end of the evening and Dan was touched when he said, 'I'm going to be eighteen next Saturday and we're having a bit of a bash here. You're invited if you like, Father.'

Dan couldn't believe this young pale boy was so old. He thanked Tony and said he would try to come to the party, at least for a short time. Then he asked, 'Are you still at school, Tony?'

He laughed. 'No! I left when I was sixteen, soon as I could.'

'So what are you doing now?'

'Nothin'. I can't get no job. Sometimes I busk a bit, but I can't get a real job. I'm out of work, like me dad's been for years.' Then his face brightened. 'But it's all gonna change now, Father. I'm gonna join the army, as fast as I can.'

Dan reacted without thinking. 'Oh, no, no, Tony, don't do that!'

'Why not?'

'Well, surely you don't want to get involved in fighting, killing people, do you?'

'All I know is that I want to do something. I want out of here. I don't want to be like my dad.'

'But there must be something else you can do? Go to college? Learn a trade?'

'Nah, I can't do them things. I'm stupid, Father. I can read, yeah, but that's about it, 'cept for my guitar, of course.'

'But what do your parents think?'

'Me dad don't really care, but Mam wants me to go. She wants me to make somefink of myself. She said she would be dead proud of me if I was a soldier.'

'Tony, it's nothing to do with me, but I do urge you to think again, please.'

Only two days later a couple came to see Dan. He invited them in, and they both shook their heads firmly when he offered tea or coffee. They didn't accept his invitation to sit down either. Dan realised that the woman was very angry. The man looked indifferent; he was thin, with a shaved, bony head

The woman began to speak: 'You got no business interferin' with our Tony!' she said.

'Tony? Oh Tony …! I'm very sorry if I've upset you.'

'Upset us! I should think you have. He was all set to go in the army till you put your oar in. And now 'e can't make 'is mind up, 'e's that upset!'

'Mrs Paley,' Dan said, 'please do sit down, both of you.' They didn't, so he struggled on, 'Look, I'm sorry, very sorry if I've upset Tony. And you're right, I was quite wrong to interfere. I just couldn't bear the thought of him having to fight and kill people.'

'Oh, you couldn't bear it, then? Well, how do you think it is for us? How do you think I can bear it , month after month, year after year, seein' 'im doin' nothin' except strummin' that guitar, no money, no job, no hope? Our Tony's a good lad, 'e deserves to make something of 'is life and then you, what 'as nothin' to do with 'im comes along and tries to put 'im off. Come on, Jeff,' she said to the man who was presumably Tony's father, 'we've been and said it. We can go 'ome now.'

Dan watched them go, feeling pity for them and very conscious of his own inadequacy.

It was only a week later that Basher came round to the presbytery. 'You never came to Tony's party,' he said.

'Oh, Lord, Basher, I forgot. I'm sorry. Did it go well?'

'Yeah, it was cool, man. You would've liked it.'

'Are you OK, Basher? You don't look too happy?'

'Nah, it's Tony. 'E's gone.'

'Gone?'

'Yeah, gone to join the army. Is that crazy, man, or what? I told 'im not to go, I begged 'im, Father, but it's 'is Ma, she's …'

'Yes, I know,' Dan said. 'I'm sorry, really very sorry.'

'Yeah, it's a bad day, Father. But I thought you should know. 'E liked you, see. Thought you was cool.'

CHAPTER THIRTY-FOUR

It was not many days later that Dan got home to find Jeff and Sylvia Paley on his doorstep. He had only to glance at their faces to know that something dreadful had happened.

'Tony?' he asked.

'Yes, 'e's dead. Killed at Catterick. 'E died in an accident in training. They said they was very sorry.' Jeff choked out these words and Sylvia held on to him, sobbing. Dan managed to get them inside, where Peggy brought them tea.

'We should of listened to you, Father,' Sylvia said, wiping her eyes. ''E was our only child, you know. 'Ow could we 'ave let him go?'

After a while Jeff spoke again. 'We're not Catholics, Father,' he said, 'I'm not sure what I believe. But we came to ask could you do Tony's funeral for us in your church?'

Hilary Clough's funeral was long delayed, as Bill wanted to wait until her godson, travelling in Bhutan, could be contacted. The young man arrived in Barnham the same week as Tony was to be buried.

The two funerals could hardly have been more different, but for those like Dan who grieved for the loss of Hilary and felt deeply for the family, and at the same time grieved for the loss of Tony and felt deeply for his parents, it was a dreadful week.

Hilary had made the arrangements for her own funeral. She asked that people should not wear black, but cheerful, colourful clothes. The congregation honoured her wishes, but no amount of bright clothing and lively music could lessen the deep sadness that pervaded the atmosphere.

The church was full; more than twenty people were standing at the back. It was a beautiful, dignified, intensely sorrowful service.

Two days later, it was Tony's turn. His was a tight-knit family that kept to themselves. They had few relations and even fewer friends, and they had specifically asked that Tony's regiment would not be represented.

When Dan walked into the church, robed and ready to begin the service, he was dismayed. It seemed unbelievable that the boy the local paper had proclaimed a hero should be so pitifully mourned. He was angry with himself. He should have given Jeff and Sylvia more guidance, found someone to help them choose the music and bring flowers.

Ashamed and miserable, he was about to begin the service when the main door of the church crashed open and in came Basher and his band, Cody and Susie and Glen and several other young people Dan didn't know. Basher waved to Dan and shouted, 'Hey, man, wait a minute!'

Dan couldn't help smiling. And although it took almost to the end of the service, both Jeff and Sylvia eventually managed a weak smile too.

Dan was able to do the basics of the funeral service in among the songs and prayers contributed by the Youth Group. Cody read a poem she had written. It didn't rhyme and it didn't scan, but it reduced everyone present to tears. Basher played the drums very well and a boy called Greg played the guitar badly. The girls did their best to sing in tune, but it wasn't easy to hear the words of their songs.

When the undertakers appeared at the end of the service, Susie went up to Jeff and Sylvia. 'The boys want to carry Tony out,' she said, 'if it's all right with you.' Jeff nodded and Sylvia's eyes filled with tears yet again.

Basher, Glen, Greg and another boy hoisted the coffin onto their shoulders with difficulty, guided by the chief undertaker, and slowly made their way down the aisle, followed by Tony's parents and family. Dan stepped into the sacristy and made a quick call to Peggy, before joining the mourners at the grave. The short service was soon over and before anyone could drift away, Dan said, 'Everyone is welcome to come over to the presbytery now. Please do come.'

Jeff was holding Sylvia by the arm, and Dan took the other. 'Are you all right? he asked the couple.

They both nodded and then Sylvia spoke. 'It was lovely, Tony would 'ave been so 'appy. We didn't know 'e 'ad all these friends.'

'I hope you'll come over to the house?'

'Yes,' said Jeff, 'yes, thank you. We'd like to thank those kids.'

Luckily there was a supermarket just round the corner from the presbytery and Peggy had managed to hurry round there to buy two large bags of teacakes and chocolate biscuits. She had only just got her breath back when the funeral party arrived. There was enough food and drink for everyone, and the Paleys were not left alone for a moment. They were the last to leave and as Dan watched them walk away he made a mental note to keep in touch with them.

Later it occurred to him that a number of the young people should have been at school, or in some cases at work. He decided it would be wiser to ask no questions.

That evening, when Peggy had gone home and the house was empty, his spirits sank again. It had been a terrible week, commemorating two such tragic events. In a moment of uncharacteristic superstition, he wondered if he should expect a third disaster.

However the following day, something quite different happened.

CHAPTER THIRTY-FIVE

Dan was lingering over breakfast, scanning the local paper,when there was a ring at the door. He opened it to find three people on his doorstep, a tall young man with tousled hair wearing a faded corduroy jacket, a pretty young woman with hair close-cropped like a boy's and, fast asleep in a bag that was slung round the young man's neck, a very new baby.

For a second or two Dan was just smiling the usual smile of welcome that he gave to strangers, then recognition dawned and he cried, 'Rupert! And Imogen! Oh, what a lovely surprise! How wonderful! But come in, come in,' Dan was laughing with joy, and now, looking at the baby he said, ' Is he – she – yours?'

Imogen laughed, 'Of course,' she said, 'and he's Daniel, after the nicest person we know – at least he will be when you've baptised him. That's what we've come for.'

'I couldn't be more delighted,' said Dan, 'but why on earth didn't you tell us?' He'd had no word from Rupert, except for occasional postcards from Africa and South America since the wedding over a year ago and had prayed for these two often. There had seemed so little hope for Imogen and Rupert, and yet …

'We wanted it to be a surprise,' said Rupert.

'But where are you living? What are you doing? Oh, it's so good to see you!' The words came tumbling out of him, and just then Peggy arrived. She hugged them both and cooed over the baby. 'What a surprise!' said Peggy. 'Does Kate know you're here?' Imogen laughed. 'No, we've kept Danny a secret. But we're taking him round this afternoon.

Peggy brought them some coffee and then hurried back to the kitchen determined to make a lunch they would all remember.

'Now tell me what you've been up to,' Dan said. 'I can't wait to hear your news.'

'Well, we want to hear about you and St Bon's,' Rupert said, 'but okay, we'll go first. He glanced at Imogen as if to say, 'Over to you'.

'We're living in an ecumenical community,' she began. 'We went there as soon as we came back from our travels. Rupert's father found it for us. Rupert does the gardening, and he's fast becoming an expert.' Dan couldn't help glancing at Rupert's hands, once so white and smooth, now roughened and brown.

'But I'm actually training to be a youth worker,' Rupert said. 'I do the study in the evenings and I've already had one or two placements in the area. My experience with the Youth Club here stood me in good stead and I really love the work. So we hope to stay in the community for another year, until I'm qualified. Then I'll try to get a job.'

'That's excellent news,' said Dan, 'and what about you, Imogen?'

'I do my share of the housework in the community and I'm training to be a spiritual director. And of course Danny takes up a lot of my time.'

'We have two chaplains in the community,' Rupert said 'an Anglican and a Roman Catholic. They're both very nice and both pretty old, quite long retired, I think. We can get to daily Mass, which is a blessing of course, but we don't want anyone but you to baptise Danny.'

'You will, won't you, Dan?' asked Imogen shyly. 'He's called after you.'

'I can't think of anything I'd like to do more' said Dan.

CHAPTER THIRTY-SIX

One day when Dan was immersed in paper work he heard the doorbell ring. Seconds later, Peggy poked her head round the study door. 'It's Kate Moriarty,' she said pulling a sympathetic face. Dan grinned. He knew Peggy found Kate rather trying, although they were both such good women in their different ways. Kate was in a hurry as always and refused a cup of tea or coffee.

'I know I'm always badgering you, Dan, but I do feel strongly about so many things.' The apologetic approach was unusual. 'Don't worry,' Dan said. 'Thank God there are people like you who do feel strongly about things. How can I help you, Kate?'

'It's the Justice and Peace Group,' she said. 'It was going so well a couple of years ago, but now we seem to be getting nowhere. There's hardly ever more than five or six of us at a meeting, and think it's a disgrace in a parish the size of ours. People just don't seem to care.'

'What would you like me to do?' asked Dan.

'I'd like you to preach about it – you know, a really strong sermon getting through to people that we're all responsible for the oppressed and the underprivileged, urging them to join our group. Could you do that?'

'I could try,' Dan said, 'but wouldn't it come better from you? I could preach a very short homily and then you could have, say fifteen minutes at the end of Mass.'

'Thanks,' said Kate, 'I would have loved to. But I know very well that lots of people don't like me. I'm too brash and aggressive. No, they'd listen to you, Dan. Will you do it for me, please?'

Dan took a long time preparing the sermon but in the end abandoned his notes and spoke from the heart. The following evening he had a phone call from Kate.

'Thanks, Dan,' she said, 'your sermon was great. I've already had six people asking to join the Justice and Peace Group. Now we'll really be able to get something off the ground.'

He had hardly put the phone down when the door bell rang. It was Joe Conroy, a gifted teacher. 'I'm sorry to bother you, Father,' he said, 'but I'd just like to ask your advice.'

'Come in, Joe, it's good to see you. How can I help you'

'Well I found your sermon yesterday very moving and it made me want to join the Justice and Peace Group.'

Dan's face lit up. 'Excellent, I can't think of anyone better. Kate will be delighted.' 'Well, thanks,' said Joe, surprised and blushing, 'but you see there's a bit of a problem. I already go out four nights a week – I belong to Amnesty and the Housing Committee and the SVP, and I'm learning to do counselling.' 'Stop!' said Dan, laughing. ' Are you asking me if you should join the J&P Group on top of all that?'

'Well, I did wonder if God wants us to have a bit of relaxation,' said Joe. 'You see I have quite a bit of preparation work for school, too. But as you know I'm not married and have no dependents, so I feel I should give all the time I can.'

'That's great,' said Dan. 'But I'm absolutely positive God wants us to relax and enjoy ourselves some of the time. Can you spare half an hour now to relax with me and have a drink?' Joe smiled. 'I'd love to, Father, some other time perhaps. I promised to visit an old lady at the Lawns Nursing Home.'

Halfway to the door he stopped and turned round, looking at Dan quizzically. 'I wonder how much relaxation you get, Father?' he said.

CHAPTER THIRTY-SEVEN

When he had gone Dan went back to his study and began to write some letters. After a while he put down his pen and sighed. Maybe Joe's right, he thought. Maybe I should set aside some time for myself and take a day off and stick to it, get some exercise and fresh air.

It was some years since he'd played any golf, but he decided to take it up again. He joined the local golf club. The course was a few miles out of town, in beautiful countryside, and after a few Wednesdays spent out there Dan felt healthier and more relaxed. He made several new friends, including Jeremy Waite, a doctor who was a Catholic and had recently moved into the parish with his family.

One day Jeremy asked him, 'Do you ever play squash, Dan?'

'No,' said Dan. 'I've never tried it. But I'd like to.'

'Good, when could you come down to the club?'

'I'm afraid it'll have to be Wednesday evening, it's the only free evening I have.'

'That's fine,' said Jeremy. 'Why not come down tonight? I can lend you the kit.'

Dan soon got the hang of squash and found it exhilarating. Some days he played golf, some squash, and occasionally both on the same day. Sometimes on a Wednesday evening he went to the theatre or to see a film. At first he felt a little guilty but quickly came to realise that he was refreshed and better able to cope after his day off, and he found himself looking forward to Wednesdays.

He tried to be ruthless and take his day off come what may, but sometimes it just wasn't possible.

One Wednesday in September, William O'Connor, his oldest parishioner, was to be buried. There was nothing much Dan could do about that, and in any case he was very fond of William and was glad to be the priest at his funeral. A coach load of cousins and other relatives had flown over from Ireland for the occasion and they pressed him to join them for lunch. It seemed ungracious to refuse and he spent an hour and half with them. Returning to the presbytery he found two notes. The first read:

Dear Father Dan,
Just to remind you that Jean Litherland, the Quaker, is coming to talk to the Unity Group tonight.
Yours Janet.

Oh, Lord, thought Dan, I'll have to go. It's only polite. That means I'll have to miss the film – oh well!

The second note was scribbled:

Father, I've got to see you. I can't wait here. Please come here to 11 Grafton Street as soon as you can.
Dorothy Wells.

Dan hardly knew Dorothy but there was an unmistakable urgency in the note. He drove round to Grafton Street. It was in a run-down part of the town, and many of the houses were derelict. The street was sunless, the houses tall and grimy. At number 11 the woodwork was rotting and the door had not been painted for years. The net curtains were yellow with age and grey with dirt.

In answer to Dan's knock, the door was opened by Dorothy. He hadn't seen her for some time. She was white-faced and wild-eyed, her hair hung lank and greasy to her shoulders, her thin cotton dress fitted her badly and her legs were bare.

'Oh, Father, come in, thank you, thank God you've come' she said.

They were standing in the hall passage. A door opened

ahead of them and a grim-faced woman came through. She glared at Dan and said in sneering tones, 'Who's this then? Your fancy man?'

Dorothy said nothing, but tears welled in her eyes. 'Will you come upstairs, Father?' she whispered. Dan nodded and began to follow her. The old woman gave an evil cackle. He smiled down at her. 'Good afternoon, madam' he said politely. For a moment she was taken aback and stood, staring up at him, then she turned abruptly and slammed the door behind her.

Dorothy led Dan into her bed-sitting room. It was warm and tidy. In a carry cot on the floor a baby was sleeping, beautifully dressed and obviously well cared for.

'Is this your baby?' Dan asked.

'Oh, yes,' said Dorothy, smiling for the first time. 'Isn't she lovely? I've called her Christine.' Then she broke down.

'Oh, Father, I love her so much. She means the whole world to me, but I've hurt her badly. She's a battered baby! Look ...' Gently she pulled up the blanket and showed Dan the sleeping child's leg. There was a vivid purple bruise along one thigh.

Dan was horrified and altogether puzzled. 'What happened, Dorothy?' he asked.

She began to cry again, and spoke between sobs. 'I married Jimmy last year,' she said. 'It was a terrible mistake. I thought I loved him but I didn't really know him at all. We had no money and we couldn't get a council house so we came here to live with his mother – that's her downstairs. Christine was born nine months after we were married, but Jim had already left me. He's gone off with a girl – she's a typist where he works, and I haven't seen him since. He never even came to see Christine when she was born.

'His mother hates me and she wants me out but I've nowhere to go. And you see, Father, Christine won't settle at night. She cries and cries and I just can't do anything. She keeps Jim's mother awake and she shouts at me and tells me it's all my fault and I'm no good as a mother. I get so tired, Father, I would just lose all hope except for her.' She paused to look at the baby.

'She's lovely, Dorothy,' said Dan, 'and you obviously take great care of her.' It was the wrong thing to say.

' But I don't ! ' Dorothy cried passionately. 'I told you - I hit her last night, the poor little thing. I'd just got her to sleep and Jim's mother came in, drunk. She slammed the door and started shouting. Christine woke up and started crying again and I just couldn't bear it any more. I saw red and I hit her. As soon as I had done it I nearly went mad. I think I would kill myself if it weren't for her. I can't see any way out. The nurse will be round tomorrow – she comes every week. When she sees Christine's leg she'll have her taken into Care, I know she will. And I don't blame her, but I can't bear it, Father. Oh, what am I to do?'

For answer, Dan went over to the sofa where she was sitting and put his arm round her and held her close. She cried for a long time, then at last she drew away from him. 'I'm sorry,' she said.

'Don't be silly,' said Dan. 'Can I make us a cup of tea?'

As they drank it he said, 'I think the first thing we've got to do is get you and Christine out of here.'

'Oh, can you? Will you? That would be wonderful!' she looked at him wide-eyed.

Dan looked round the shabby room at the wretched young woman and the beautiful sleeping baby. 'I promise you, Dorothy, you'll be out of here tonight,' he said.

CHAPTER THIRTY-EIGHT

Dan spent the next three hours trying to find accommodation for Dorothy without success. At six-thirty he remembered that Bill Clough chaired the housing committee, and phoned him. Bill was silent for a while, thinking hard, 'There's nothing official I can think of, Father. I'm sorry. But there's just one person who might help. She's not a Catholic.'

'I don't care if she's a Hottentot or a Red Indian,' Dan said. 'Who is she?'

'Lady Paula Sinclair,' said Bill. 'She lives in a cottage on her son's estate out at Binkley. She's eccentric but generous and there's just a chance she might take Dorothy in.'

Dan drove out to Binkley. He found the cottage easily from Bill's directions – newly white-washed, thatched, surrounded by a well-tended garden. He couldn't imagine anything more different from 11 Grafton Street.

An old woman answered the door to him, invited him in and listened to his story. 'Bill Clough thought you might be able to help', Dan said. 'He didn't say how.'

Lady Sinclair smiled. 'Yes, Bill phoned to tell me you would be coming, and he gave me an outline of the situation. I expect he knows I have a weakness for waifs and strays,' she said. 'Unfortunately I've got a family from the East End of London staying here this week, but they'll be gone by Monday and your Dorothy and her baby could move in then.'

'What, do you mean, here?' Dan was astonished. 'But you don't know her.'

'Well, I know Bill Clough, and I know you a little bit

156

now, Father Spring,' she said. 'And I do try to see Jesus Christ in everyone, though sometimes,' she added with a twinkle, 'it's jolly difficult. From what you say I'll have no problem with Dorothy, and it won't be too lonely for her. I'll see she gets involved in the village. If she's young and strong and willing, she'll be a Godsend for me. I'm too old now to look after this place properly.'

Dan drove as fast as he legally could on his way to Dorothy. But as he turned into Grafton Street he remembered his promise: 'You'll be out of here tonight.'

He sighed and shrugged. Minutes later he was in Dorothy's room. 'Well, are you and Christine packed?' he asked.

She surprised him. 'Yes, Father,' she said. She had washed her hair and was wearing a clean dress. 'Right,' he said, 'You're coming to stay at St Bon's till Monday and then you and Christine are going somewhere rather like Paradise.'

When they got back to the house, Dan looked at his watch and saw it was five to eight. He told Dorothy to get some supper and asked her to make up a bed in the spare room.

Then he went off to listen to the Quaker at the Unity Group. The woman spoke well and as Dan listened he found the simplicity of the Friends' way of worship very attractive. The meeting was long and three people wanted to speak to him afterwards. When he got back to the presbytery he found Dorothy in her dressing gown, smiling. Christine was miraculously asleep.

Dan was too tired to eat – he said goodnight and stumbled wearily to bed. So much for my day off, he thought. The phone rang; the voice was distraught. 'It's Mollie Waite, Father. Jeremy's dead. He had a heart attack after playing squash. Can you come, please?'

He went.

The following month, Dorothy came to see him, with

Christine in a pushchair. Lady Sinclair had driven them into town. One look at their faces and there was no need to ask how they were.

'How is Lady Sinclair?' asked Dan.

'Paula?' said Dorothy, 'she's fine. She's like a mother to me and she dotes on Christine.' Dan was delighted. At least I've got something right for once, he thought. Then he noticed to his surprise that Dorothy seemed nervous, embarrassed.

'Is there something troubling you, Dorothy?' he asked gently.

'Well, yes, Father, there is,' she began. ' Oh, I feel awful about this, you must believe me.'

'Of course I believe you. But what is it?'

'Well, you might have noticed. I haven't been to Mass since …'

'Since you went to live with Lady Paula. But that's perfectly understandable. I wouldn't expect you to come all this way. And in any case there's no public transport. But I'm the one at fault, Dorothy. I should have got someone to bring Communion out to you, or come myself.'

'No, no, Father,' Dorothy was really distressed now, wringing her hands and keeping her head down, 'it's not that. You see, I've been going to church with Paula. There is a lovely little church in our village, and the vicar's ever so nice. The service is nearly the same as ours, and I know it's awful after all you did for me, but I've decided to become an Anglican!'

She forced herself to look up and saw to her surprise and relief that Dan was smiling.

'Well, Dorothy,' he said, 'I think I should congratulate you. That must have been a tough decision and I guess in your circumstances it's the right one.'

'You're not offended?' Dorothy asked.

'No, and much more importantly, I think I can assure you that God is not offended either. What matters is that you continue to love him and love the people in your life. Now, I know Peggy is biting her nails in the kitchen, longing to see little Christine again, so off you go to show her off!'

Half an hour later, when Dorothy had left, Peggy came into his office, clearly upset about something.

'The cheek of it!' she said. 'I couldn't believe my ears!'

'What? What's happened to upset you, Peggy?'

'Upset me! I should think so! That young Madam, and after all you've done for her!'

'You don't mean Dorothy? Why? Oh, I see. You think she shouldn't have left the church?'

Peggy stared at him. 'You seem so calm. Don't you mind? Aren't you hurt?'

Dan laughed. 'No, Peggy, I'm not hurt in the least. Just sit down and think for a moment. Think about all the young women in Barnham, of a similar age to Dorothy. How many of them go to any sort of church? We have to face it, we live in a post-Christian age, at least in this country. So I think it's good news that someone like Dorothy takes her belief in God so seriously, and I'm sure his kingdom is wide enough to embrace us all.'

But Peggy was not entirely convinced. She stomped away, muttering about ingratitude.

CHAPTER THIRTY-NINE

When Wilfrid Drew came round to tell him that Lydia was divorcing him, Dan was very surprised and deeply shocked. Although each in their different ways quite often irritated him, Dan had always thought of them as the epitome of reliability and decency. Besides, he was fond of them both.

Wilfrid accepted the whiskey Dan offered him and began: 'Oh, Father, it was such a shock . It was terrible. Even when I heard her, I just couldn't believe it.'

'How did you find out?' Dan asked gently.

'We have two phones, you see, and just by chance I picked up the one in my study when Lydia was on the other line and the first words I heard her say were "I'm going to ask your father for a divorce." The shock was terrible, Father, and I began to shake. I knew I should have put the phone down but I felt I must hear what she was saying, so I sat down and went on listening. She was talking to Abby – Abigail, our daughter, I think you've met her, and you can imagine how I felt when I heard what she said to her mother. She said, 'Good on you, Mum! I've often wondered how you put up with Dad for so long – he's such a boring dry old stick.'

Wilfrid stopped and took out a handkerchief. Dan felt an immense pity for him.

'Are you sure you got it right? Are you sure that's what Lydia and Abigail said?'

'Well, I'm not sure if I've remembered the exact words, but I think I have. You have to admit they're fairly unforgettable!'

'Did you hear any more of the conversation?' Dan asked.

'Oh, yes,' Wilfrid sounded bitter now. 'I heard my daughter, my daughter I've always loved so much say, "Go on, Mum, tell me. Who's the lucky man?" It was so callous, I just felt I couldn't believe my ears. And I couldn't bear to hear any more, so I put the phone down.'

Wilfrid lifted his glass to his lips and took a gulp of whiskey.

'Will you help me, Father? I just don't know what to do. Please come and talk to Lydia, persuade her to see sense. We've been married for nearly thirty years, and I've always tried to put Lyd first. I've never been unfaithful. But I know I can't get through to her!'

'Have you tried?' Dan asked.

'Oh yes, but it was hopeless. At first she was furious with me. She said I had no right to eavesdrop on her private conversations, and she thought I would never sink as low as that.'

Dan tried not to show his surprise, but he thought, this is intolerable. I never imagined Lydia could be like this.

But Wilfrid had finished his whiskey, and went on, 'Then she changed. I think she's really sorry. She said it just happened out of the blue, she had never considered leaving me, but when Sebastian came into her life, she just couldn't help herself. "He's so wonderful, Wilfrid," she said, "he's just right for me, just what I want. But I never wanted to hurt you, you've always been so good to me. I'm truly sorry you had to hear like this."

'I suppose it was inevitable, Father, but we were soon having the most awful row. Like I said, I just couldn't make her understand how I feel. But I think you could. I think she would listen to you. She's always been such a staunch Catholic, so critical of people who get divorced. Will you come and see her, Father, please? I would be eternally grateful.'

Dan sighed. He poured Wilfrid another whiskey, then said, 'No, Wilfrid, I'm sorry but I don't think I can. I don't think it would be right for me to interfere. The days when the parish priest was expected to solve everybody's problems are long gone. This is a matter which only you and Lydia can sort out. I am truly sad, Wilfrid, that you've been hurt so badly, and I sincerely hope that this will eventually turn out to be just a blip in what has been a long and faithful marriage. And as for Abigail, well, please don't take her words to heart. I don't think that young lady is thinking very clearly. I remember when you walked down the aisle together at her wedding, and I recall thinking what a close and loving relationship you had with your daughter.'

Wilfrid attempted a smile. 'Are you sure you couldn't just come to see Lydia?' he asked.

'I'm sure,' Dan said. 'But for what it's worth, you and Lydia too will be in my thoughts and prayers.'

Wilfrid got up to go.

He looked utterly miserable.

'Come on, I'll drive you home,' Dan said, 'and by the way, you have another daughter, don't you? Catherine, isn't it?'

Now Wilfrid did manage a smile. 'Yes, there's Cathy,' he said. 'I phoned her and she's coming home tomorrow.'

CHAPTER FORTY

Cathy didn't waste much time. The following afternoon she telephoned Dan. He didn't think he had ever met her, but he liked her voice.

'Father Dan?' she said, 'it's Cathy Drew. I'm only here for one day, but please could I come to see you?'

'Yes, of course,' Dan said, 'four o'clock would be fine.'

He was sure, when he saw Cathy through the window, that he hadn't met her before. Abigail looked very much like her mother, but this young woman had very different features. She was not as pretty as her older sister, but Dan liked her serious, open face and the wide smile she gave him when he opened the door.

She held out her hand to him. 'We haven't met, Father,' she said, 'I was in Canada when my sister got married. But my parents talk about you quite a lot, so I feel I know you a bit.'

Dan couldn't recall a time when Wilfrid or Lydia mentioned Cathy, though Lydia had plenty to say about Abigail. She declined Dan's offer of tea or coffee. 'I'll come straight to the point,' she said. 'You will have guessed that I've come about Mum and Dad. Father, I know I'm young and not very experienced, but I'm so hoping this is all going to turn out to have been a silly mistake. I know my parents are very different from each other, and I can see that my mother, especially never having had a job, must have found life very dull at times. My dad is not an exciting person, but he's a truly good man and I love him dearly. I just can't bear to see him so hurt.'

'I agree with everything you say, Catherine, but I can't quite see why you've come to me.'

Her voice rose and he saw tears in her eyes. 'I've come because I need you to help!' she said. 'They both respect you, and the whole church thing means so much to them. Last night I tried and tried talking to Mother, but I got nowhere. You're our only hope, Father Dan. Please help us, please come and see my mother!'

Dan was about to give a firm refusal when the face of Deirdre Mulligan came into his mind, another young woman in distress, and he remembered how he had failed her. He had said 'It's up to you' and washed his hands of her, and she had lost her life.

'All right, Catherine,' he said, 'I'm not sure it's the right thing to do and I'm pretty sure it's not really any of my business, but I will come and I'll do my best.'

'Oh, thank you! Thank you so much! I'll never forget this,' Catherine said, and went on eagerly, 'When can you come? Can you come now, this afternoon?' Dan couldn't help laughing. 'No, I'm sorry, Cathy, the earliest I could manage is tomorrow afternoon.'

'I understand' she said, 'you must have all kinds of de-mands on your time. But I have to go back tonight so I won't be there when you come. So could I ask you, please, to phone me after you've talked to my mother? And I think it would be better if you didn't give her any warning of your visit. I know that might sound a bit mean, but I think you'll get through to her more easily if she hasn't, as it were, prepared a defence.'

Dan sighed. 'You may be right' he said. 'Look, Cathy, I'll do my utmost to make this situation less unhappy, but I'm afraid I can't hold out much hope.'

After the young woman had left, Dan spent a consider-able time in prayer. Then he went out to fulfil his various engagements. That night he slept badly, and next morning he found himself distracted more than once during the Mass at St Boniface's, a celebration he usually looked for-ward to and enjoyed. At lunch, he didn't do justice to

Peggy's steak pie, and afterwards he crossed over to the church and sat very still trying to pray.

CHAPTER FORTY-ONE

At the Drews' house Dan rang the bell and Lydia opened the door. She greeted him effusively and drew him into the sitting room. To Dan's dismay, a middle-aged man sat sprawled on the sofa. He didn't get up but smiled lazily.

'Father, this is a friend of mine, Sebastian French.' Lydia said, and then, 'Seb, this is our local priest, Father Daniel Spring.' Dan said, 'Hello there,' and Sebastian languidly waved a hand and said, 'Hi.'

Dan looked at him. The word 'smarmy' came unbidden into his mind, and he remembered that he should try to see Christ in everyone.

With Sebastian, this was not an easy task.

Lydia left them, saying something about getting tea, and the two men looked at each other. Neither was intimidated by what he saw. To Sebastian, Dan appeared of little interest, a big Irishman with no dress sense. To Dan, Sebastian seemed rather pitiful. He was clearly a good few years younger than Lydia. He had thick fair curly hair, a large loose mouth and small eyes. He wore a smoking jacket and a cravat, which seemed faintly ridiculous to Dan.

They spoke about the weather, and then Sebastian began to talk about his work. He was a theatre producer, hoping to put on a play in Barnham. Both were relieved when Lydia returned with a tray on which were tea things and a chocolate cake.'

'Darling, you're simply amazing,' Sebastian said, reaching for a slice of the cake Lydia was cutting.

Dan spoke firmly. 'Lydia, I've come to see you,' he said, 'about a private matter.'

She answered him sharply. 'Anything you want to say to me, Father, you can say in front of Seb.'

But to Dan's huge relief, the man got up, grabbed another slice of cake and made for the door saying, 'Count me out, honey, I've no interest in church stuff.'

Lydia was all smiles now. 'Do you like him?' she asked, and Dan suddenly felt pity for her. She seemed like an eager little girl, but he couldn't bring himself to answer her question.

'Lydia, I've come to talk about this question of divorce,' he began. 'I know I have no right to interfere ...'

Suddenly she snapped. 'No, you certainly have no such right! It's nothing whatever to do with you. How dare you poke your nose ...' She broke off and began to cry.

Dan waited. Eventually she composed herself.

'Father, can you possibly understand? Oh, I hope you can. You see I'm so incredibly happy! I feel young and alive again! Sebastian is just marvellous: he's the soulmate I never had. Oh, I know we had a good, solid marriage, Wilfrid and I. He was always so kind and considerate, but oh, so dull and frankly, boring. Nobody knows what I've had to put up with for nearly thirty years! But now I have my chance of happiness, and not you, or Wilfrid, or the church, or silly little Cathy are going to spoil that! I'm in love, Father, but I don't suppose you could understand that?'

Dan said nothing for a moment. Then he said, 'I do understand about being in love, Lydia. But I also think that we often misunderstand the meaning of the word "love". We mistake infatuation for love, or sexual gratification, or even perhaps imagining that we have found a soul mate.'

'Please don't preach to me, Father. The church has always meant so much to me, and I think you would admit that I've tried all these years to be a good Catholic, a good wife, a good mother ...' 'Yes, indeed, I know, Lydia, you've done all that. Which is why ...'

'But don't you see, everything's different now! I feel wonderful!' She blushed. 'Sebastian thinks I'm beautiful. He says I'm beautiful! Can you imagine how that makes me feel? Never once in thirty years did Wifrid tell me I'm beautiful!' She began to cry. Then she pulled herself together. 'You're wasting your time, Father Dan. Nothing, nobody, will dissuade me from leaving Wilfrid, from marrying Sebastian, from starting a whole new life. My mind is made up. Oh, I'm sorry for Wilfrid, and I'll miss all my friends here and I know I've upset Cathy. I also know what a serious thing it is to break up a marriage. So I'm going into this with my eyes wide open. And I am going, I'm leaving all this behind, and I'm a very happy woman.'

Dan walked slowly home. 'I was totally out of my depth,' he thought. 'I failed and I failed miserably. Perhaps I was wrong to go.' But he felt an enormous surge of pity, and yes, love welling up within him: for Wilfrid, for Cathy, and especially for Lydia. Wilfrid and Cathy would grieve for a long time, probably Wilfrid would never fully recover, but he would eventually be able to pick up a full and active life, but as for Lydia …?

CHAPTER FORTY-TWO

It was a sunny morning and Father Dan set off early on a round of visits. He had been five years at St Bon's now, and visiting the housebound was still one of his favourite duties.

His first call was to Amos Hartley, who since William O'Connor's death was the oldest parishioner. He was a gentle, frail old man who had lost none of his intelligence or interest in what was happening both in the world at large and in St Bon's parish. As always he welcomed Dan warmly, but today there seemed to be an air of excitement about him. His hands trembled quite violently as he poured Dan a cup of coffee, but somehow not a drop was spilt. Then he painfully lowered himself into a chair, took a deep breath and said, 'I've had an idea, Father!'

'Oh, yes, tell me, Amos,' said Dan with unfeigned interest.

'Well, it's for ecumenism, Christian Unity. I've been thinking and praying a lot about it. It seems to me that the best way to unite people is to give them a common cause. Y'know, I have a young niece, she's in her fifties. She's a nun in Peru, working in a hospital. Sister Martha's her name. They need money desperately. So I thought, why not get all the churches together to work to raise money for this hospital?' His face was alight with enthusiasm.

'There are all sorts of things they could do together. And, another thing, music is a great uniter. There could be a big concert of praise with music from all the churches, so that everyone could rejoice together and at the same time raise money for Sister Martha!' he leaned forward eagerly. 'What do you think, Father?'

'Amos, I think it's an absolutely marvellous idea – two marvellous ideas in fact. If only you were fit enough to put it all into operation! Have you any thoughts as to how we could get it going?'

'Well, I know there is a Unity Committee in our parish, but I'm not sure how lively it is. And I don't know about the other churches. I think it needs one dynamic person to start the thing moving and then we'll be well away.'

'Have you anyone in mind?' Dan asked. ' I can think of quite a few dynamic people but they're all up to their ears in other things.'

'Do you know David and Rosemary Bluett?' the old man asked.

Dan frowned. 'I'm sure I've heard that name. Oh, yes, they're new people aren't they? Peggy, who cooks for me, is one of the welcomers and she told me about them.'

'Well, I think he, and perhaps Rosemary too, would be just the people we need. They're not involved in anything yet, you see. They live down the road, only a few doors away. They moved in ten days ago, and they've been in to see me every day since. I can hardly believe my luck. They've already done so much to help me – mending things, shopping, the library, posting letters – and they're not bossy or interfering. I think you'll find them a real blessing, Father.'

After he left Amos, Dan went to call on the Bluetts. David was at work, but Rosemary welcomed him into a bright untidy sittingroom where two-year-old twins were playing with bricks on the floor. Dan welcomed Rosemary to the parish and then told her of his conversation with Amos.

'You've been wonderfully kind to him,' he said.

'But he's such darling old man,' said Rosemary. 'And I think his idea is great. I know I can speak for David – we'll gladly get the whole thing started. We'll need lots of help of course.'

CHAPTER FORTY-THREE

When Dan eventually got home from his visiting, as so often long past lunchtime, he found a pile of mail on the table including an airmail letter which he opened first. As soon as began to read, he realised it was from Kevin Saunders.

Dear Father Dan,

I'm writing to you during my last week in Bolivia. I've been here for the past two years and it's been the most rewarding time of my life. In some ways I can't bear to leave, but now I feel certain that I am being called to the priesthood.

I think you will remember that I came to see you about three and a half years ago. I wanted to try my vocation then, but you suggested I should try some other experiences first. I took your advice. I left the office were I was working and went to L'Arche, where I lived in community with the people with severe learning difficulties for nine months. That was good – I didn't like leaving there either! But Bolivia has been even better.

I'll be back in St Bon's parish at the end of June. This letter is just to prepare you. I am so much hoping that I can go the bishop with your blessing.

Yours in Jesus Christ,

Kevin.

Dan was delighted. The Saunders family had moved away from the parish soon after Kevin had been to see him and he'd had heard nothing of them since. He had often wondered about Kevin, and prayed for him, and especially at the time of Kevin's departure thought that perhaps he had not been sufficiently encouraging. He wrote at once to the address he had for Kevin in England, inviting him to stay for a few days.

The change in the young man was amazing. Physically he was bronzed and fit, taller and broader, but more importantly, he had lost his shyness and timidity. There was a quiet strength and confidence in him which Dan sensed immediately. Within hours of Kevin's arrival, Dan felt certain that here was a man with a true vocation to the priesthood, and he gave him a letter to take to the bishop.

CHAPTER FORTY-FOUR

Kate Moriarty was spending two mornings a week at Milly Ryan's house. Milly's husband, John, had recently died of cancer and she was finding it hard coping with two boisterous little boys and four-year-old Harriet who had cerebral palsy. Harriet was a beautiful child; she was lively and responsive but had great difficulty in controlling her limbs. Tim went to school, Charlie to a nursery where his mother Milly worked every morning. So Kate took charge of Harriet and pushed her three times a week in her wheelchair to the hospital for physiotherapy. It was working well, and once or twice Harriet had taken several steps without falling over.

The little girl struggled with speech. It was very hard for her to make herself understood. There was a speech therapist at the hospital, but she was overworked and often off work with stress. Kate asked everyone she met if they knew of a good speech therapist, but nobody did.

Kate was confident that Harriet would soon be walking, but the speech was more of a problem, and Kate felt she needed concentrated, professional help.

At Mass on Sunday she found herself sitting next to someone she didn't know, a bright-faced young woman with boisterous twins, who really smiled at the sign of peace. As they came out of church Dan grabbed her arm and said, 'Don't run away, Kate, I want you to meet Rosemary and David Bluett, and Sam and Joey.' It was the family she had sat next to at Mass.

'Could you take them down for coffee?' Dan asked. Kate hesitated. She wanted to write some Urgent Action letters for Amnesty before she made the family meal, and in the afternoon she had promised to go round to the convent to help Sister Lucy and Norah McGinty pack up some parcels of blankets and woollen garments they were sending overseas. She saw Dan was looking her sternly in the eye, and remembered what he had said when she went to confession last time: 'Slow down, Kate. You're a very good woman and your heart is big enough for the lot of us, but you need to give time to him as you well know. Don't take on everything, don't spend your life rushing from pillar to post ...' He was right of course. Tilly could perfectly well make the Sunday lunch.

'OK, Father you win!' she said with a grin, and she led the Bluetts down to the crypt. Over coffee Kate said, 'I suppose it's a full-time job looking after the twins?'

'You could say that,' Rosemary laughed. 'But I sometimes miss my job. I was a speech therapist.'

Kate's eyes opened wide.

'But that's marvellous! That's a miracle!' said she who wasn't even sure she believed in miracles.

'How do you mean?' Rosemary asked.

'There's this little girl, Harriet, you see, she's four and she has cerebral palsy. I've been helping her a bit, taking her to hospital for physio. But we've been desperate to find her a speech therapist, and now you ...'

Kate stopped, dismayed. Rosemary had stood up, leaving her coffee half drunk.

'No, no, I'm sorry, I can't help you,' she said, turning away quickly. Without a word, but smiling apologetically, David scooped up the twins and followed her. Kate stood up, intending to go after them, but thought better of it and sat down again, feeling bewildered. I've been so stupid, she thought, I've put my foot in it, taken her for granted. But she seemed so nice ... She shrugged. No miracle, she chided herself, back to square one.

The following afternoon Kate's phone rang. The voice was hesitant.

'Kate? It's Rosemary Bluett. Look, could I come to see you?'

'Yes.' Kate knew she sounded curt but didn't care. 'When were you thinking of?'

'Any evening would be fine for me. David's home then. But only if it's convenient ...'

Kate interrupted. 'Right,' she said. 'I'm free this evening. Eight o'clock.'

'Thank you,' Rosemary said meekly. 'I'll be there.'

After Kate hung up she began to feel ashamed of her coldness. After all, the woman's probably coming to apologise and explain, she thought. So after supper with the family, she lit a fire in the sitting room and prepared coffee and biscuits.

She opened the door to Rosemary with a smile. When they were seated and drinking the coffee, Rosemary began:

'Look, Kate, I behaved appallingly yesterday. I can't apologise enough. But if I could try to explain?'

'Sure, go ahead,' said Kate, 'and don't worry. Nobody in this parish has behaved appallingly more often than me!'

'I'm afraid I get very emotional,' Rosemary began, 'Comehow I just can't help it since Lily ....'

'Lily?'

Rosemary took a determined grip on herself.

'Yes, Lily was our first baby, before the twins.' She gulped. 'She had cerebral palsy, and she would have been four like your Harriet. But she died, and I wasn't there. My mother was in the house at the time, but it wasn't her fault, it wasn't anybody's fault, it was a cot death. But no matter what anyone says, I still feel, "If only I'd been there. If only I hadn't left her".'

Kate said nothing, but one look at her face showed Rosemary how she felt.

'So when I had the twins I made up my mind that I would never leave them alone. Oh, I know it's silly. I'll have to leave them one day. And I can relax if David's with them. But when you told me about Harriet, and then I realised you wanted me to treat her, and I thought it would mean leaving the boys and I didn't know if I could face a little girl like that …' She began to cry.

Kate let her cry, but when Rosemary started to apologise again she stopped her.

'Don't be silly, Rosemary. I'm so, so sorry you've had to go through all that, and are still going through it. I can't imagine how I would cope if … but you mustn't worry about Harriet. She's making great progress with her walking and she's a determined little soul. As for the speech therapy, something will turn up eventually, I'm sure. I'm afraid impatience is my besetting sin, well, one of them.'

'You're very understanding,' said Rosemary, 'but last night I had a long talk with David. And he thinks I should at least give it a try. I could come to Harriet after David's home from work (one of the blessings of living here is that he's home by five o'clock) or her mother could bring her to me once the twins are in bed. What do you think?'

Kate was silent, thinking. She knew she had a tendency to rush at things.

'Maybe it would be best if you just met Harriet first. We could have a tea-party, say next Saturday or Sunday. You could bring Sam and Joey, and I'll get Milly, that's Harriet's mother, to bring Tim and Charlie, her little boys, as well. Then we could see how it goes and take it from there. But Rosemary, I want you to know there will be absolutely no pressure on you.'

CHAPTER FORTY-FIVE

That afternoon when he was alone in the house, Dan had a telephone call. It was the bishop asking him to come to Bishop's House the following day. He sounded serious and Dan felt slightly apprehensive. But the bishop was cheerful and welcomed him kindly. In his study he pointed to an armchair and told Dan to relax.

'I've got some news you may not like, Dan,' he began.

'Oh!' Dan steeled himself to face whatever it was.

'I'm going to move you from St Bon's.' 'Oh, no!' Dan couldn't help his vehement response. 'Where are you sending me, John? And why, for heaven's sake?'

The Bishop smiled. 'I'm giving you a plum job,' he said, 'chaplain at the university!'

'Oh, please, no, John,' Dan was dismayed. 'I beg you, don't send me there.'

'Why ever not? I thought you'd be pleased.'

'Look, John, I don't think it's at all a good idea. In the first place, I didn't go to university myself. I'd feel out of my depth there. And more importantly, the students wouldn't take kindly to having a fifty-nine year old chaplain. Don't you see, I'm practically an old man! And I'm so happy at St Bon's. Or is there something I'm doing wrong there?'

The Bishop couldn't resist smiling at Dan's extreme reaction. Then he said, 'Look, Dan, of course you've done nothing wrong. On the contrary, you've done wonders for that parish. But I know the signs all too well. You're tired and you're stressed. The chaplaincy job won't last for ever, but it will give you a break. You should find life considerably more restful.'

'But...' Dan began. The Bishop ignored his interruption. 'Hugh Marshall has run the chaplaincy long enough.

He's done a good job there but he needs the challenge of a big parish. So I'm simply going to swap the two of you, and I'll brook no argument!' Dan saw he had no option, and decided to give in gracefully. 'Your will be done, my Lord,' he said with a grin.

'Before you go, Dan, I want to thank you for all you've done these last few years. I know you've worked far beyond the call of duty and you've improved the lives of a lot of people.'

The acknowledgement was welcome, but it did little to cheer Dan. He decided to stop in Rowan Street on the way home.

Agnes welcomed him as always, but seeing his face as he stepped inside, she asked, 'What is it Dan?'

'I'm to be moved' he said. 'I'm to be the university chaplain!'

'Oh!' Agnes sat down and for a moment there was silence between them. Then she said, 'I'm sorry, but I'm glad too. I shall miss you badly, we all will, but we need people like you to work with the young. How do you feel?'

'Oh, Agnes, I don't want it. I never realised until now how happy I am here, how rooted I feel. I don't know if I'll be any good as a chaplain.'

'Well,' said Agnes, 'I've often noticed that a lot of teenagers contribute well to the parish, but when they go off to university, we hardly see them in church again. So it will be a wonderful challenge for someone like you, who will see that they continue to lead vibrant Christian lives.'

'Put like that, it does seem worthwhile but, as you say, a challenge.'

Smiling she said, 'You'll manage, I know you will! How have the people taken the news?'

'You're the first person I've told, Agnes. It seemed right – you've been a dear friend to me over the years. I'll be grateful if you'll spread the word for me.'

As soon as he had gone, Agnes walked across town to the lane where the Bluetts lived, and told them her idea.

'Fine,' said David, 'I'll see to it, Agnes.'

CHAPTER FORTY-SIX

When Dan got home he found Nancy and Pat Slater on his doorstep. He visited the Slaters quite often, knowing life was tough for them. Pat was unemployed, except as a casual labourer, and the house was full of children. He didn't ever remember the Slaters coming to see him. He guessed it must be something pretty important.

Once inside, Pat came straight to the point. 'It's our Peter, Father.' 'Oh, yes? He's number three isn't he? Red hair and freckles?'

Nancy smiled. 'That's right, Father, and full of mischief he is. But we've got a big problem.'

'Oh dear,' said Dan, 'I hope he's not in trouble?'

'No, no, Father, it's nothing like that,' said Pat. 'No, but it turns out Peter has more brains than the rest of us put together. Lord knows where he gets them. Us Slaters was never scholars.'

Nancy was smiling to herself, and Dan guessed that she was a woman of some intelligence.

'The thing is,' Pat went on, 'Mr Wykes at the school took him over to the Cathedral School at Fenchester, and they tested his voice and it turns out he can sing like a nightingale. The long and short of it is, Father, Mr Wykes says he can easily get a scholarship to the Cathedral School. They have small classes there, he says, and it would be a great chance for Peter. There's even transport laid on, and we would have help with the uniform ...'

'He's not going!' Nancy's voice was quiet and firm.

Dan was surprised. 'But why not, Nancy?' he asked. 'It sounds a wonderful opportunity to me.'

'But it's not a Catholic School, Father!' Nancy was near to tears. 'Surely you are on my side?'

Dan laughed. 'I'm not on anyone's side, Nancy. I just think there are other ways that Peter could keep up with his religious education. Sister Lucy is excellent at this, and in a family like yours he's surrounded by people who love God. If he were my son I wouldn't hesitate to send him to the Cathedral School.'

The words 'if he were my son' made a sharp impact on Nancy. Near to being overwhelmed by the demands and needs of her own family, she had never given much thought to those who for whatever reason were childless.

She said nothing.

Pat looked at her hopefully. 'Nancy?' he said.

'Well, I'll think about it' she said.

The two men exchanged a wink, and Dan was touched to see how much his son's education meant to Pat.

A month later in the summer holidays, Peter Slater came to serve the weekday Mass and in the sacristy afterwards he took a crumpled letter out of his pocket and handed it to Dan.

'Me mam said to show you this,' he said.

It was a letter informing the Slaters that Peter had won a scholarship for the Cathedral School.

'Congratulations, Peter!' Dan said. 'What does your Mum say?'

Peter's freckled face split into a wide grin. 'She says she'll skin me alive if I get big-headed or stuck-up,' he said.

CHAPTER FORTY-SEVEN

Many people had thought it was too ambitious to hold the Evening of Praise in the Town Hall's vast Assembly Room, but as it turned out, it was packed to capacity – people were standing in every available space. The organisation had been superb. In the front row, upright in a wheelchair, sat Amos Hartley, who had never dreamt of actually being present.

It was an occasion for worship and for enjoyment too. The Anglican Rector, Canon Forester, spoke for two minutes about the hospital where Sister Martha worked, and a young Indian girl from the URC Church spoke for three minutes about Christian Unity. There was music to suit everyone: a gospel choir, Bach on the organ, Wesley hymns, charismatic choruses, the Salvation Army band, St Bon's Youth Band and a solo by Peter Slater.

Dan thoroughly enjoyed himself. His taste in music was catholic and, although he couldn't sing himself, he was able to appreciate everything. He was also glad that for once he had no official part; he was just one of the crowd. The last item was 'The Church's One Foundation,' and he stood up to join in with a full heart.

He thought this was the end and saw to his surprise that he was mistaken. Philip Best, the Methodist Minister, who was a good friend, came up onto the platform and raised his hand. He's going to bless us all, Dan thought.

But Philip said, 'Could I ask you to be seated, please? At least,' he added with a smile, 'those of you who can.'

When people were seated he said, 'This has been a wonderful evening and an occasion this town will long remember. Our thanks are due to Mr Amos Hartley, for it was his idea in the first place, and to those who organised everything – they have done a superb job. But before we go, there is something else that needs to be said: Father Dan, where are you? Can you come up here?'

Dan felt himself colouring, felt people pushing him forward. He had been standing at the back, and as he made his way to the front, people began to clap. By the time he reached the platform the whole crowd was singing 'For he's a jolly good fellow.'

Then Philip spoke again. 'I think everyone here knows Father Dan is about to leave us. Of course it's good news for the university that they are going to have so excellent a chaplain, but it's sad news, not just for the parishioners of St Boniface's, but for all of us here tonight. We are going to lose a good priest and a very good friend.'

'Oh, Lord!' thought Dan, 'I feel like crying! What am I going to say?'

But all eyes had turned from him to the edge of the platform where Glory Tattershall was helping two small bundles on to the stage. It was four-year-old Rosie Mulligan and Harriet Ryan, also four years old.

Rosie, flushed and smiling broadly, held a bunch of flowers in one hand and was holding very tightly on to Harriet with the other. Slowly and carefully they made their way across the stage to where Dan stood. There was absolute silence. Rosie held the flowers up to Dan; Harriet's words came out shaky but clear enough for all to hear, 'Thank you, Father Dan.'